# He Will Go
# FEARLESS

# He Will Go
# FEARLESS

## LAURIE LAWLOR

SIMON & SCHUSTER BOOKS FOR YOUNG READERS
New York   London   Toronto   Sydney

SIMON & SCHUSTER BOOKS FOR YOUNG READERS
An imprint of Simon & Schuster Children's Publishing Division
1230 Avenue of the Americas, New York, New York 10020

This book is a work of fiction. Any references to historical events, real people, or real locales are used fictitiously. Other names, characters, places, and incidents are products of the author's imagination, and any resemblance to actual events or locales or persons, living or dead, is entirely coincidental.

SIMON & SCHUSTER BOOKS FOR YOUNG READERS is a trademark of
Simon & Schuster, Inc.
Book design by Christopher Grassi
The text for this book is set in Palatino.
Manufactured in the United States of America
2 4 6 8 10 9 7 5 3
Library of Congress Cataloging-in-Publication Data
Lawlor, Laurie.
He will go fearless / by Laurie Lawlor.
p. cm.
Summary: With the Civil War ended and Reconstruction begun,
fifteen-year-old Billy resolves to make the dangerous and challenging
journey west in search of real fortune—his true father.
ISBN-13: 978-0-689-86579-4
ISBN-10: 0-689-86579-1
[1. Fathers and sons—Fiction. 2. Dogs—Fiction. 3. United States—History—
1865–1898—Fiction. 4. Overland journeys to the Pacific—Fiction.] I. Title.
PZ7.L4189Heaw 2006
[Fic]—dc22
2005006129

For Chauncy

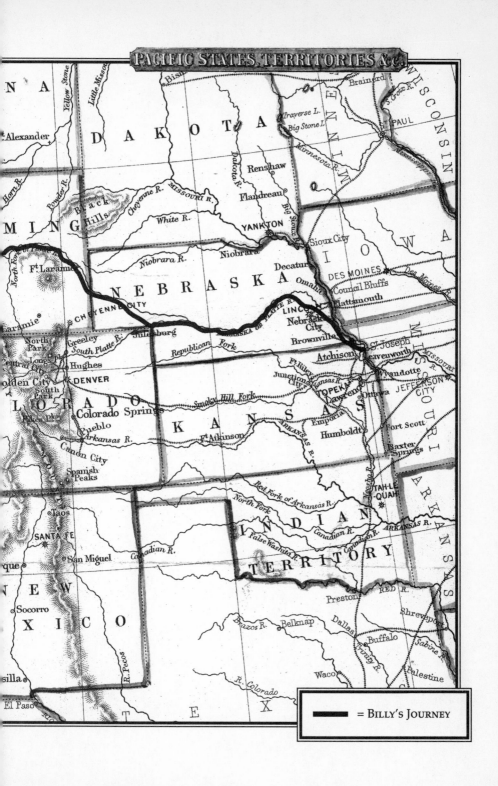

PACIFIC STATES, TERRITORIES &c.

= BILLY'S JOURNEY

He will take the wildest steer in the world,
   and break him and tame him;
He will go, fearless, without any whip, where
   the young bullock chafes up and down the yard;
The bullock's head tosses restless high in the air,
   with raging eyes;
Yet, see you! how soon his rage subsides—
   how soon this Tamer tames him. . . .

—Walt Whitman,
"The Ox Tamer"

# Chapter One

———◆•◆———

"CATCH THAT PIG, WILL YOU, MISTER?"

A small black-and-white blur careened past Billy. The pig stretched out its stubby front legs, whirled its hind legs, and barreled straight for the river. The pig's owner, a pretty, young woman in a sunbonnet, stood on a nearby hill, waved her apron, and wailed at the top of her lungs.

Just as Billy was about to drop his valise and give chase, two strangers who had been idling at the water's edge tore off their fancy stovepipe hats and rushed toward the bristly fugitive. "Here, pig! Here, pig!" the stockier fellow shouted as he waved his hat in the air.

"Don't just stand there, Rock. Grab him!" commanded his companion, a young man in a shabby black frock coat.

"How come I always got to do the dirty work? Jackson, you grab him."

The sly pig dodged left, then right. With long, silky ears

flying, the squealing creature slid through the mud and hurtled into the Missouri. *Splash!*

Shocked and wet, the yelping pig twisted and streaked back up the embankment straight for Billy. The young woman screamed. Billy lunged. The pig snorted, showed the whites of its black eyes, and bared its sharp teeth. Before Billy could get a good grip, the slimy creature wriggled free and darted between his legs.

With crazed determination the pig hurtled full speed toward Rock and Jackson. They clapped their hats back on their heads and flapped their arms up and down like big, useless wings. "Here, pig! Here, piggy-pig!"

The pig swerved out of reach, circled them once, twice, then shot along the riverbank and headed upstream.

"Run!" Rock and Jackson shouted to Billy.

Billy pivoted, stretched out his long, ungainly legs, and took off after the pig. At first he ran with a gangling gait. He pumped his knobby elbows, thrusting his arms through the air like a drowning man. His breath felt jagged, forced, and he was conscious of the screaming and shouting of the crowd gathered at the shore. But after a few strides he stopped hearing Rock, Jackson, the girl, or the crowd. His breath found its own natural rhythm, and his legs moved with singular grace. With every long stride he felt new, hidden strength in the muscles of his calves.

The pig, as if sensing it was going to lose the race, feinted to the left and headed back the way it had come. Billy circled around too. With a flushed face and thick black hair plastered with sweat, he grinned like a maniac.

"Here, pig! Here, piggy-pig!" Jackson shouted.

The pig shot under a nearby empty wagon. For a moment nothing happened. The pig seemed to have vanished.

Jackson signaled to Rock and Billy. He motioned with his hands to surround the wagon silently on three sides. They crept closer. Suddenly Jackson leaned over, cupped his hands to his mouth, and howled, "Here, pig! Here, pig!"

The ambushed pig streaked out from under the wagon. Rock was ready. He took a flying leap, tackled the pig, and held fast to its pumping hind legs. The pig screamed as if it were being murdered. "Help me, will you?" Rock shouted over the ear-piercing din.

Without even pausing to think, Billy slipped off his best coat and threw it over the pig. Jackson scooped up the furious animal, wriggling and thrashing inside the sweaty coat. He swaggered up the embankment with the pig under his arm. "Here you go, miss," Jackson announced in a gallant voice. "I hope your creature's none the worse for wear."

The young woman's broad grin revealed two rotten front teeth. "Thank ye," she said, and giggled. She grabbed the snarling runaway. Jackson tipped his elegant hat as the girl hurried toward a line of wagons waiting to cross the Missouri on the next ferry.

"Coulda ate that pig," grumbled Rock. He brushed dirt from his arms and elbows. The seams around the shoulders of his worn coat seemed to strain under the bulge of muscles. The dingy paper collar around his thick neck had been torn in several places. His tie was missing, and his unshaven, pockmarked face was streaked with dirt. With disgust he retrieved his dented hat from a puddle.

"A ham dinner would have been delicious," Jackson admitted, "but it wouldn't have been very chivalrous." He handed Billy his filthy coat. "You're some runner. Thank you for assisting a poor young lady in distress. Quite attractive, except for the teeth."

Rock rolled his eyes. "Don't go starting again, Jackson. You know what happened last time. Her pa's got a shotgun, like all the rest."

"A minor detail." Jackson used his handkerchief to dust off an overturned barrel. He took a seat and removed one of his fashionable patent-leather boots. His big toe stuck out of his threadbare sock. He carefully tucked a piece of folded newspaper inside the shoe, then began to scrape away pig manure from the nearly worn-through sole. As he completed this fastidious operation, he glanced up every now and again, as if to study Billy. "Rock, return our new friend his hat. We could use somebody like this fellow. Fleet of foot, resourceful, tireless."

Rock sighed and scooped up Billy's dusty plug hat from the ground. "Sorry this don't look so good anymore. That was a mighty hot chase. Name's Rock, and this is Jackson. Who are you, and where do you come from?"

For a moment Billy felt taken aback. "Nobody," he wanted to say. "Nowhere." Instead he flapped his coat to knock away some of the mud. "Name's Billy. Lived on the Missouri all my life." He decided that was enough to tell these strangers. To keep from looking at Jackson, Billy glanced toward the dock, where the steamboats had begun loading. He was so busy studying the crowd of emigrants he didn't notice Rock wander away.

"Billy, are you in some kind of hurry?" Jackson asked in a

friendly voice. He pulled a small comb from his breast pocket and carefully began to groom his fine, pale mustache.

"No, sir." Billy tossed his battered hat in the air and caught it, again and again, just to show he had all the time in the world. Secretly, however, he was calculating how many minutes remained before his stepfather would return from his noon dinner. Just like clockwork—the same as every day—he'd unlock the front door to Butcher Furniture and Caskets, march inside, open the safe, and carefully count the morning's receipts. When he noticed the missing money, there'd be hell to pay.

Billy grinned, imagining how his stepfather would stomp and bellow and pound his meaty fists against the wall. For once he'd have to take his anger out on the plaster, not Billy.

*Click!*

Startled, Billy dropped his hat.

"Kind of jumpy, aren't you?" asked Jackson, who had just snapped open a tin of mustache wax. "How old are you, Billy?"

"Nineteen," Billy mumbled, and stood up straight. His tall, lanky frame and serious expression had often fooled people into thinking he was much older than fifteen.

Jackson arched one eyebrow. "You in some kind of trouble, Slyboots?"

"Me, sir? No, sir."

"How come you aren't in school?"

"No particular reason." Billy narrowed his dark eyes. He didn't like to be called nasty nicknames—especially by nosy strangers. "School's out." The truth was that he hadn't been to class in more than a year—ever since that spring day when he tossed his hat out the half-open window of the suffocating classroom. When the teacher told him to retrieve it and return for his whipping, Billy climbed out the window and never went back. The only thing he had tolerated about school was recess. He was the fastest runner in the school. Nobody had ever beaten Billy in races they held in the field behind the schoolhouse.

"Got a job?" Jackson demanded. He dipped two fingers into the mustache wax.

"Did have one until the circus was closed down. Trapeze accident. I lost three brothers in that act." Billy paused, fascinated by the way Jackson pinched and twisted the ends of his mustache into two neat curls. For the past year he had studied the pictures in the *Morning Herald* advertisements in hopes that one day he'd have a fine mustache. "I'm thinking of finding some other line of work. Nobody wants a tightrope acrobat these days."

"Where you headed, Billy?" Jackson asked in a friendly voice. He slipped the tin back into his pocket. "Tell me the truth this time."

Billy squirmed. "Upriver, then out west."

"You going overland?"

"I reckon."

"Dangerous Indian country between here and Virginia City."

Billy's face began to turn red. "How do you know where I'm going in Montana Territory?" Nervously he followed Jackson's gaze. "Hey!" he shouted when he spied Rock waving his steamboat ticket in the air and then rifling through his valise. "What do you think you're doing?"

"Awful lot of gear you got packed here," said Rock. "Socks, comb, soap, knife, change of clothes, picture glued together of some old feller. Cowboy, maybe."

Billy clenched his fists. "That's private. Give it back."

Nimbly Jackson intercepted the photograph, which looked like a reassembled puzzle pasted to a piece of cardboard. "Does this gentleman know you've run away from home?"

"Ain't running from home!" Billy bellowed. He could feel the unstoppable, humiliating burning grow around his eyes, his cheeks. Billy Blush. How he'd always hated that taunt.

"If you ain't running from home," Rock said, grinning, "then what are you doing?"

"Now, Billy," Jackson said in a mocking, fatherly way as he waved the picture in the air, "don't you know that running away from yourself is the hardest thing to do?"

Helplessly Billy swiped his eyes with the heels of his dirty hands. Everything was going wrong. All wrong. He had always prided himself on the way he kept the upper hand, pilfering small change from younger, weaker boys—the ones who accidentally insulted or irritated him or his friends. How had he been so stupid, so careless to step into a trap he knew so well? "Look here, fellows," Billy pleaded, trying his best to sound manly and cajoling at the same time, "that picture ain't none of your—"

"Here we go, Jackson," Rock interrupted. "This is our lucky day." He shook a small cloth bag tied at the top with string. *Ching, ching, ching.*

Billy charged full speed at Rock. He threw himself against the burly fellow. Rock didn't budge. He just chuckled and dangled the money in the air. "Give it!" Billy shouted, gripping Rock around his waist. "Give it back!"

Jackson crossed his arms in front of his chest, then calmly examined his fingernails. "How much?"

Billy hurled himself again at Rock. Nothing happened. Rock seemed as rooted to the spot as a massive cottonwood. Sweat streamed down Billy's face. A sick, sinking feeling twisted inside his gut. This was hopeless. His clothes had been ruined, he'd been humiliated, and he'd been robbed. He didn't dare go to the sheriff. Not with his record. Now how would he ever get out of Saint Joe? He was penniless. Escape was impossible. His life was over. He might as well turn himself in right now.

In desperation Billy begged, "Please, don't take all my money. I'll do anything." His voice sounded as unnatural and high pitched as the squealing pig after it had been trounced by Rock.

"*All* your money, Slyboots?" Jackson scoffed. "Who ever said we'd take all your money?"

Rock stopped jingling the bag. He gave Jackson a menacing look. "I thought—"

"Now, now!" Jackson interrupted. "Let's be civilized." He stood up, strode closer, and snatched the bag from Rock's reluctant fingers. He opened it and counted the money carefully. "Looks like about twenty-nine dollars."

"Twenty-nine dollars and two bits," Billy said defiantly. He straightened his shoulders, hoping he looked a bit more threatening. "I stole it from a safe. There was piles and piles of cash."

Jackson shot a glance at Rock. "Billy, you're telling us that you cracked a full safe? My dear friend, why didn't you take *more* money?"

"Well, I . . . I—"

"Don't misunderstand. This is a considerable sum," Jackson interrupted. "We are impressed. There's certainly enough here for you to entertain the idea of partnership in our excellent venture. The kind of enterprise that will make you richer than your wildest dreams."

"You want to make me your partner?" Billy demanded in a mistrustful voice.

"Absolutely." Jackson casually tossed the bag of money back to Billy. "This is your lucky day, Slyboots."

Billy clutched the money bag tight to his chest. Stunned and grateful, he didn't dare breathe.

"Now, Jackson, wait just a minute," Rock protested. "You promised we'd just go halves."

"Well, we're going thirds now," Jackson said, and smiled beneath his mustache. "That's even better."

Rock looked puzzled. "It is?"

"Absolutely. By inviting this fine young gentleman to be our partner, we have leveraged our risk. We have increased our capital potential. We have broadened our horizons, and we have vouchsafed our perpetuity. We have in fact, dear Rock, exceeded our wildest expectations—all because this young man will provide us with the wherewithal to float upriver on the next steamboat leaving for Nebraska City and will guarantee that we will not starve. Am I correct, Billy?"

Billy nodded tentatively. "You mean you're not going to rob me?"

"No!" Jackson said, and laughed. He clamped Billy on the shoulder and then added in hushed tones, "You are coming with us to Montana Territory to one of the richest claims ever worked on Alder Creek. You, my friend, are about to become a very wealthy man."

Billy gulped. "I am?"

"Absolutely. And better yet, you will achieve stupendous fortune in the company of two veteran travelers who happen to be excellent shots. Is that not correct, Rock?"

"If'n we can find spare firearms and bullets," Rock said in a glum voice. "With thirty cents between us, we can't hardly afford—"

"A minor detail!" Jackson fluttered one hand in the air.

"Wouldn't be boring traveling with you fellows," admitted Billy. He had always preferred associating with tough, reckless outcasts who made his parents cringe. Secretly Billy liked to think that he belonged to a family of bad brothers of his own choosing. Rock and Jackson were undoubtedly the oldest, wiliest, and most worldly of any devilish companions he'd ever known. "You seem to know your way around."

"Billy, not only will we protect you against dangers on the road to Virginia City," Jackson said in a low, confidential voice, "but we are offering to let you in on our secret."

"I thought," Rock grumbled, "we agreed to never tell nobody about that."

"Flexibility is the mother of invention. Never say never," Jackson replied. "Read him the notice, Rock."

Reluctantly Rock fished from the inside of his boot a creased, greasy piece of paper. He glanced over his shoulder as if to make sure that no one else might be listening. In a hesitating voice he read aloud: "'One hundred teamsters wanted for the Plains. Virginia City destination. Apply at intelligence office on Francis Street, between Second and Third Streets.'"

"A fabulous opportunity!" Jackson exclaimed when Rock was finished reading. "All that is required is one dollar and fifty cents for each of us. A kind of finder's fee to our future employer. And then all we have to pay for is my fare and Rock's on the next steamboat north to Nebraska City. From there we'll be driving wagons west into the very heart of the Montana goldfields, where you can scoop up a bushel of gold nuggets big as melons in an afternoon. We will be guaranteed a safe, reliable, and easy way to travel west at the same time we'll receive a salary."

Rock licked his lips. "Tell him how much, Jackson."

Jackson smiled. "Twenty-five dollars a month."

"Brilliant plan, ain't it?" Rock said. "Driving a wagon's nothing. Jackson and I drove a wagon through most of the war. Being a teamster was the easiest job in the Union army."

"So, what do you say, Billy? Will you join us?" Jackson asked. "We have some very reliable information about how to make a huge sum of money very quickly. Enough wealth so that I can return triumphantly to the open arms of my fiancée and her rich, blue-blooded family in Vermont. And Rock can build himself an enormous mansion and live in peace and security and—"

"Jackson, you swore you wouldn't—," Rock interrupted in a threatening voice.

"Don't worry. I'm not going to reveal all the details." Jackson cleared his throat. "Let's just say, Billy," he whispered, and handed Billy his steamboat ticket, "there are many individuals who would like to get their hands on our *m-a-p*." He nodded knowingly and winked.

"That's enough!" Rock said with a flushed face. He crossed his beefy arms in front of himself. "You say one more word and you're a dead man."

Jackson cocked his head. "Now, now, Rock. We're among friends, aren't we? Take a deep breath. Count to ten. Maintain your equanimity."

Billy gulped. Rock's rage made Billy as nervous as Jackson's charm. "Can I please have my picture back?" he asked.

Jackson nodded. Billy tucked the photograph and all his other precious belongings into the valise and snapped it shut. Quickly he stuffed his steamboat ticket into his pocket. In the distance he spied a line of covered wagons moving slowly toward the ferry dock. Time was wasting. He couldn't risk lingering here any longer and being spotted by the authorities. "All right," Billy said finally. "I'll go with you. On one condition."

"Name it," Jackson said.

"*I* handle the money," Billy replied.

Jackson grinned. "A perfectly reasonable request. We'll be a trio, how's that? Stampeders with style. Let's shake on it, partners," he said, holding out his hand. One by one they each solemnly shook hands.

*Dong-dong-dong.* The steamboat bell tapped the familiar warning Billy knew meant last chance to board. "Hurry! There's not a moment to lose," Jackson said. He adjusted his hat on his head and pointed to their trunk. Rock hoisted it onto his shoulder.

Billy followed the two young men as they sprinted toward the dockside steamboat office. Billy pulled his hat down as far as he could on his forehead and lifted his coat collar. "Two fares to Nebraska City, please, sir," said Billy. He spoke in a low voice and kept his head tilted downward so that the clerk might not recognize him.

"Eleven dollars total. You can board the *Denver*. She's leaving in two minutes," the clerk said. He took Billy's money and passed him the tickets.

Billy barely had time to retie the money bag and stuff it inside his pocket before Jackson grabbed him by the elbow and shook him hard. "Run!" he shouted.

# Chapter Two

━━━◆◆◆━━━

"AAALLLLL ABOARD!"

The steamship bell tapped three times. Billy, Rock, and Jackson were the last to climb on deck before the steamboat ramp was removed. The side-wheeler rumbled, and the water churned noisily as the *Denver* nosed into the main current and headed upstream.

"You boys wait right here," Jackson said, then disappeared.

Rock and Billy dropped the trunk and valise and slumped wearily on the deck. Leaning against the trunk, Rock pulled from his pocket a small brown bottle of Parker's Ginger Tonic. He pushed back his hat and took a long swig. "Ain't you gonna wave good-bye to Saint Joe?"

"Nope," Billy replied, glancing at the tonic. The last thing he wanted was to appear odd. Some kind of pitiful, homesick baby. "Are you ill?"

"Not much," Rock said, and smiled. "Parker's Ginger is the best health and strength restorer. Want some?"

Billy shook his head.

"You don't look so good, Slyboots."

Billy felt his cheeks burn. "Never felt better in my life."

"Suit yourself." Rock took another swig, then dozed.

Billy pulled the valise closer for safekeeping. He sniffed the river's familiar smell: an infusion of decay—loam and rotting leaves, fish heads and soggy wood. He knew the river in all seasons. In the spring the Missouri rumbled and groaned, burst its banks and ran wild and powerful, raucous and violent. Piles of deadwood and reefs of bloated cattle corpses jammed downstream. In summer the river flowed sullen and low. By late fall and early winter the gray-black water crackled with ice that eventually froze as hard and silent as iron. Whatever time of year, the river taunted him with the possibility of escape.

Back in Saint Joe he had worked in his stepfather's store after failing and running away from school. He had spent ten hours a day imprisoned indoors stacking boards, sorting nails, oiling hinges, and dusting caskets. While he was trapped like a snag half-buried in mud and gravel, everything exciting in life seemed to flow past him on a swift current. Eager emigrants swarmed into town for supplies to "see the elephant"—to go on a perilous adventure west, where many hoped to make a fast fortune in the mines. Every day he had had to listen to Saint Joe veterans who lingered outside the store describing to each other their exploits at Antietam and Gettysburg— glorious combat in a war that had ended before Billy was old enough to enlist. How soon before all the gold was prospected?

How long before every chance for bold, heroic action vanished?

A few weeks earlier, when the ice finally broke, Billy had looked out through the open doorway of his stepfather's store and heard the whistle of the first steamboat heading north. At that moment he felt a surge of terrible restlessness as powerful as the rush of crying geese flying overhead, following the curve of the riverbank north. And he knew he had to get away—or die.

The steamboat whistle shrieked, jolting Billy out of his thoughts. He pinched himself just to make sure he wasn't dreaming. He really *was* heading upriver. Carefully he studied the passing shoreline, which he vowed he'd never see again. The steamboat floated slowly past the low-hanging trees where he had spent so much time in summer with his friends, swinging and leaping into the water. There went the roof of McCosker's barn, where he'd first learned to smoke a piece of clothesline and play poker. There was the steeple of the church where he and his friends had once lifted the dismantled carriage of the minister.

Onshore Billy spied Malcolm's shack and recalled how he and his friends had tin-canned the tail of the old bootblack's dog and sent him howling down the street. He saw the back fence of the fire station and remembered the time that Charles Bradbury, the traveling scenic artist for Drake's Plantation Bitters, had come all the way from Saint Louis to decorate rocks and trees with letters and signs showing the virtues of his elixir, and how afterward Billy and his friends had painted more signs on back fences and even on the sides of cows. These were the only times in Saint Joe that Billy had felt the least bit authentic, vital, and alive.

Furtively Billy unlatched the valise. He wanted to make sure that the photograph was safe. He had studied the dashing image so many times that he knew by heart the way the man's broad-rimmed hat was pushed back jauntily on his head, and how three little wrinkles between his dark eyebrows made him look fierce and mysterious, and how his dark mustache concealed his mouth so that it was impossible to tell if he might actually be smiling. For good luck Billy circled the face once lightly with his thumb.

"Here you go, fellows," Jackson announced. "A dinner fit for kings."

Rock sat up, wide awake. Billy quickly hid the photograph and shut the valise. Jackson took a seat on the floor beside them and untied a cloth containing three stale buns, a chunk of yellow cheese, a fine sausage, and an entire fried chicken. From his coat pocket he produced a cold bottle of beer.

"Nice work, Jackson," said Rock. He began to eat with gusto, barely bothering to chew his food. Sensing that the feast would soon be gone, Billy joined in with enthusiasm. He had not realized until this very moment how hungry he was. For the first time he appreciated Jackson's generosity and thoughtfulness.

"A delicious repast!" Jackson declared. A crumb of cheese clung to his mustache. "We have our young partner to thank for this meal." He lifted the bottle to salute Billy, then took a long swallow and passed it to Rock.

"I didn't do anything," Billy said, pleased all the same.

"Oh, yes you did. Couldn't have bought this fine meal from an enterprising Mormon on the lower deck without your monetary contribution." Jackson flipped the limp money bag to

Billy. "Here's the leftover change, Mr. Treasurer. You should be more careful of pickpockets."

Billy scowled. *Outside the steamboat office.* That must have been where Jackson had filched his money after he'd paid for their tickets. Frantically Billy tore open the bag. To his horror he discovered that, thanks to Jackson's slippery fingers, there was only $12.50 left in the treasury. After they paid the $4.50 needed to start their new jobs, there'd be only $8.00 remaining. "Blast it!" Billy said. Before he could accuse his new partner of breaking his promise about the management of the money, Jackson and Rock stretched out on the steamboat deck, hats over their faces, and fell fast asleep.

Well, it was a good meal. Billy had to admit that. Contentedly he closed his eyes and dozed.

At some point in the night the *Denver* anchored in a small cove, and at dawn the next day the Missouri was shrouded with late-June mist. Wispy, ghostlike shapes formed and re-formed on the rippling brown current. The smell of wood smoke from the smokestack flooded the air.

The steamboat bell tapped three times. *Dong. Ding. Dong.*

Billy awoke with a start. A solitary heron squawked. Red-winged blackbirds threatened one another with harsh warning calls. He rubbed his eyes and waved away buzzing mosquitoes. In the confusion of so much noise, he sat up, not quite able to comprehend that he was not in his bed in his home in Saint Joe anymore. He was on a steamboat, where he'd spent the night on the hard deck using his valise for a pillow.

Stiffly he moved his head to the left, the right. He felt the lumps on his head and considered what the learned Professor

Fowler had told him when he had his skull examined for fifty cents. "Your chief organ is benevolence," the famous fortune-teller and phrenologist had said as he probed Billy's head with his long, cool fingers. "You ought to be pitched right into the river of life, and told to sink or swim and made to do your own work. You should seek your father's wisdom. Your mother lacked expectation, so that you were born with too little spirit of adventure. Please cultivate this."

Billy smiled. *"Seek your father's wisdom."* Wouldn't Professor Fowler be pleased to see him now? Just as he was about to share his premonition of good luck with his traveling companions, he noticed something odd. Rock and Jackson had vanished. Their trunk remained. *They'll be back soon.* Perhaps they had gone to look for some water to drink. Billy waited patiently.

After nearly half an hour they had still not returned. Billy began to pace. *Where could they be?* His heart pounded in his throat. *Why did they leave me?* Anxiously he patted his coat pocket for the fifth time to check for the much depleted money bag. Then he went through his valise. Nothing was missing there, either.

Billy sat down, hunched forward, and pulled his knees toward his chest. Loneliness suddenly enveloped him like a dank mist. Now what would he do? He had no idea where to find the teamster outfit once he arrived in Nebraska City. He didn't even know where to start.

He frowned. What had Jackson called them? *"Stampeders with style."* Rubbish! Billy was certain his so-called partners had jumped ship without their trunk. Rock and Jackson had swum ashore after making so many promises. Billy should never have believed Jackson's dazzling talk about rich mine stakes and a secret map. He should never have been taken in by Jackson's flattery. *"Fleet of foot, resourceful, tireless."* What a fool Billy had been to trust him! If he ever saw Jackson or Rock again, he'd give them a piece of his mind. Leading him on in that cruel way. Giving him hope that he'd strike it rich. He should never have trusted them. He should never have listened to them. He should never have—

"Rise and shine!" Jackson's strident voice called out. An apple thudded into Billy's lap.

"Where were you?" Billy jumped to his feet and grabbed Jackson by the lapels of his coat. He wanted to smash him in the face with his fist. Only Jackson's icy blue stare made him stop.

"A bit peevish this morning, are we?" Jackson removed Billy's clutching hands, then scooped up the fallen apple from the deck. "Here's your breakfast."

Billy stared at the apple suspiciously.

"It's going to be fearfully hot this morning," Jackson said. He flicked away dust from his sleeve. "Once the sun burns this mist, we're going to have to find a shadier place to rest. I have already surveyed the possibilities. There are nearly three hundred Mormon emigrants traveling on this boat, all crammed belowdecks. Not a bit of room there. The pilothouse and the officers' quarters are the only areas with suitable awnings. Sitting out in the direct sun for hours is a first-rate way to experience sunstroke. When I was in the Vermont Second Brigade, there was this soldier who nearly died from heat exhaustion."

"Do you always talk so much?" Billy demanded in a gruff

voice. He felt more irritated by his own lingering sense of panic than by Jackson's chatter.

Jackson looked surprised. "Why no, Slyboots. Perhaps river travel's made me especially loquacious."

"What's that supposed to mean?"

"Talkative," Jackson replied in a superior voice. The deck began to vibrate beneath their feet. This meant that the side wheels were rumbling forward again. Slowly the shaking steamboat glided into open water. From the deck below came the resounding cry of a baby, the deep voices of arguing men, and the piping protests of a young woman.

Jackson draped his coat over his arm. "It's time for me to fly away," he said. "If anyone asks, say you didn't see me."

Before Billy could demand to know what Jackson meant, he'd disappeared. Billy shrugged. Just as he was about to take a bite from the apple, two husky men in shapeless felt hats stormed up the stairway from the lower deck. Between them they dragged a simpering young woman in a faded gingham dress. Tears streamed down her pale face. As soon as she spied Billy, mouth agape and apple in hand, she let out a little cry.

"That him, Essie?" one of the men barked.

She stared at the apple. Before Billy could say a word, the second weasel-faced fellow shoved him hard against the railing pole. The other fellow pressed his knife against Billy's throat. The apple dropped from Billy's hand and rolled across the deck.

Billy gasped, certain that at any moment he would be slit from gill to gill like a gutted catfish.

"What? Speak up," Weasel Face demanded, "b'fore I kill you!"

"Si-thr-bin-take!" Billy said between clenched teeth. The man lowered the sharp blade slightly. Billy coughed. "Sir, there's been a mistake!"

"A mistake? Not likely! I saw you with my sister, and I mean to take revenge."

The girl began to sob. "Ain't him, Sid!"

Billy felt the blade bite the skin beneath his neck. He closed his eyes and prayed. *Please, God, don't let me die.* He thought of all the things he hadn't had a chance to do. Grow a mustache. See the world. Find his father. He was too young to die. *Can't they see who I am?*

"Ain't him!" the girl screamed again. "He ain't the one!"

The sharp pain that Billy had felt beneath his chin disappeared. Sid had stopped pressing heavily against his chest, and the wooden railing pole no longer bit into the back of Billy's skull. Billy hunched forward, his hands to his neck, and struggled to breathe again. Small white stars circled and circled before his eyes.

"You ain't him?" Sid demanded.

Billy shook his head. "Don't know who you're talking about, sir. Sir, I never saw this girl before. I've just been minding my own business."

"Ain't been dallying?"

"No, sir." When he looked at his hands, he saw a thin smear of blood on one palm. His knees began to go wobbly, and he felt that he was sinking down, down like a man drowning. Like the time he stepped into the river and the sandbar wouldn't hold him, and in seconds he was up to his knees in soft, wet sand, and even though he called and called for help, nobody came. Nobody came. Nobody—

The next thing he knew, he heard Rock's voice shouting at him. "Hey! Hey, wake up!" Somebody slapped Billy's face. Something icy splashed his cheeks, filled his ears and his eyes. Gasping for breath, he sat up, choking. Rock smacked him hard on the back. "That's better, Slyboots!"

"What happened?" Billy sputtered.

"Keeled over, I guess," Rock said, holding an empty tin cup. "I got here just when it happened. Two fellows and a gal took off fast as chained lightning. You all right?"

"Yeah, I'm fine," Billy said, too flustered to think up an outrageous excuse. His face was bright crimson. With effort he struggled to his feet and scooped up the apple. He took a deep breath, glad to be alive. "Those two fellows thought I was somebody else," he said, trying to sound lighthearted. "Something about that young lady. They said there was a scoundrel taking advantage of her. Mistook me for the one, I guess." He rubbed his neck, hoping he sounded like it was all a great joke, even though his hands were still shaking.

Rock did not look the least bit amused. "Where's Jackson?" he said darkly.

"Jackson? He was here earlier. Left all of a sudden. Before he did, he gave me this apple. Generous of him, don't you think?" Billy polished it on his sleeve. He was just about to bite into it when he noticed something that made him lose his appetite. Someone had taken a knife and neatly carved into the apple skin a heart that enclosed two initials: J & E.

Now Billy understood. *Jackson and Essie.* Jackson had carved his initials with that girl's in the apple to impress her. And look what had happened. That lying scoundrel's romancing had almost gotten Billy killed. In fury Billy curled his fists and slammed his left hand hard into the wall. The pain shot through his arm, but Billy was too angry to feel anything.

By noon the river and sky seemed to flow together like molten brass. Heat shimmered on the water. Just as Jackson had predicted, the sun's glare became almost unbearable. Billy tried his best to keep out of the way of any other angry Mormon emigrants. He crept into what little shade he could find, but soon there was none to be had on the hurricane deck. It was too hot to wear a hat or a shirt or a coat, but when he removed all three, his skin began to turn pink and blister. To make matters worse, there was nothing to drink but cloudy, muddy-tasting water teeming with creatures.

The water didn't bother Rock. He solved his thirst problem by drinking three bottles of Parker's Ginger Tonic. Nothing seemed to wake him as he snored, wrapped in his coat.

It was nearly evening before Billy saw Jackson creep back up onto the hurricane deck again with two tin cups. At first Billy refused to talk to him, even after Jackson apologized about the misunderstanding with the Mormon woman and her kin. "Have some ice water," he said, smiling. "Got it from the officers' quarters."

Billy smacked the cup out of Jackson's hand.

"Have it your way," Jackson said. He gulped the water from the other cup. "You always so angry?"

"Only when people try to get me killed by fellows who think I'm somebody I'm not."

"Would it help if I apologized again?"

"No."

Jackson sighed. Clearly the silence made him uncomfortable. "You'll never guess who I just met."

"I don't want to hear about it." Billy yanked at his collar. He was so hot he felt ready to jump off the steamboat. Why, he could have hopped on one foot, blindfolded, to Nebraska City faster than this rattletrap boat was traveling—barely three or four miles per hour. How much more of this sun and glare could a body stand?

Jackson did not seem the least discouraged by Billy's hostility. "An old acquaintance from the Vermont brigade is among the officers," Jackson continued. "My outfit and hat convinced him I was a gentleman slightly down on my luck. It's against the regulations, but he said I could have as much of the officers' ice water as I wanted. If you'd rather not have any, I won't force you." He picked up the fallen tin cup and disappeared.

Immediately Billy felt sorry for his harsh words. Sometimes his rage emerged like a sudden grass fire, the kind that couldn't be stopped until it burned itself to bare, scorched earth. When Jackson returned with more water, Billy coughed. "I *am* parched," he said in a small voice.

"Drink hearty!" Jackson said.

Billy couldn't help but smile half-heartedly. He took a sip. The cool water tasted delightful.

Gradually the heat in the air began to ebb. Billy tried to find some breeze on the hurricane deck. Unfortunately, everyone else aboard had the same idea. Families with children, the elderly, sweethearts, and surly married couples crowded up out of the sweltering lower regions of the steamboat, where the boiler seemed to scald the surrounding air.

As the sun finally began to set, someone started playing a violin. It was a mournful song, "What Was Your Name in the States?" The riverboat passed dark trees on either side. Frogs croaked. Billy glanced about the growing shadows at the crowd of strangers the way he always did. One by one he searched the faces for the man with dark eyes, dark hair. *Somebody who looks like me.*

Suddenly a deep voice called, "Billy? Billy!"

Billy felt the hair bristle on the back of his neck. He didn't dare move or look around.

A young boy, perhaps nine or ten years old, darted between two seated women. He skipped once, twice, then he called, "Over here, Pa!"

Billy's heart pounded and his hands sweated, so fiercely did he envy the boy with his name. What would it be like to be so lucky to call someone Pa in such a careless, trusting way? *"Over here, Pa!"* The words made Billy so furious he wanted to jump up and slug the boy in the face, blacken both his eyes, and give him a good kick in the stomach.

Billy could not trust himself to stay one more minute. He stood up, shoved both his damp hands into his pockets, and left the deck. Back and forth he trudged beside the railing, reminding himself again of how he had never felt as if he fit in anyplace. When he was younger, he'd assumed he was some kind of changeling, left behind in the wrong family. Tall and dark, he had towered over Ma, who was short and fair. His half brothers were squat built, plump, and pale, with blue gray eyes and white-blond hair. He didn't look like them, either.

For years before he'd been told the truth, he'd always

imagined he looked like his father. Billy's mother had told him that his pa had been a miner out west who died in an explosion the year after Billy was born. "A tragic cave-in," she always said in the same pious voice she used to read prayers or spread gossip. Then she'd clamp shut and wouldn't say another word. Since Billy had no living grandparents and nobody except a crazy, reclusive maiden aunt, there had been no way to find out more.

Billy's mother had remarried when he was three years old or thereabouts. Lots of boys Billy knew had different fathers from their original ones, mostly because of the war or diphtheria or accidents. Billy had never questioned the arrangement. It was all he knew. But he and his stepfather had never found much to enjoy in each other.

His stepfather was a hard, stubborn man, practical and unforgiving in his ways. "The apple don't fall far from the tree," his stepfather had said when he beat Billy for laziness, lying, troublemaking, or fighting. "I do this for your own good. You're incorrigible and bound for hell. Just like your pa." His stepfather always told him he was counting the days till Billy could support himself and be gone forever from under his roof.

"Well, now you get your wish," Billy murmured. The river rumbled in the darkness. "I've gone and done it, Ma. I'm gone for good."

Jackson slept atop the wheelhouse roof that night, using his boots for a pillow. Billy and Rock, both badly sunburned and sore, tried to sleep on the hurricane deck. When they awoke the next day, the sun shone fiercer than ever.

"Feel like I might roast to death," Billy said. He waved his hat in front of his bright red face.

"A pale complexion gives us away as greenhorns," replied Jackson. "Think of your sunburned skin as good preparation for the Plains. Next thing we need to do is exchange our tall hats for soft ones."

"Why we got to do that?" Rock demanded, scratching his head. "Better sunshade?"

"My dear Rock, appearance is everything," Jackson said. "We do not wish to be taken advantage of in Nebraska City, where gentlemen are disdained. We must look rugged. No one will take us seriously in stovepipe hats."

Billy watched carefully as Jackson wandered across the lower deck and approached a young man in a nearly new broad-rimmed felt hat. After only a few moments of conversation the man traded his hat for Jackson's worn-out hat.

Billy couldn't help but admire Jackson's sharp dealing. "What did you tell him?" Billy asked when he returned.

"I simply informed him of the latest fashion."

"What's a farmer need with fashion?" Rock demanded. "Your hat was pretty well used up besides."

"Never underestimate a man's vanity or his eagerness to cultivate the acquaintance of the fairer portion," Jackson replied, smiling. "I simply told him that wearing a hat like mine would attract almost any young lady."

"Horsefeathers!" declared Rock. "Here's how to trade your hat." He sauntered across the deck and approached a young man in a felt hat, rolled at the sides, with a feathered band wrapped around the crown. He pointed to the stranger's hat, then to his own. The stranger shook his head. Rock repeated the gesture. Again the stranger refused. As he was about to walk away, Rock grabbed him by the arm and seemed to be saying something to him in a low voice, the way he leaned forward. The young man turned pale, handed Rock his hat, and hurried away.

"Quick work, Rock," Jackson said. "What convinced him?"

"Threatened to kill him if he didn't make the trade," Rock replied, inspecting the excellent exchange. "How do I look?" He placed the hat on his head at a cocky angle.

Billy gulped. "Like a real Western plainsman."

"Now it's your turn," Jackson said, clamping Billy on the shoulder. "You got to trade your city hat for a Western style."

"Why? This one suits me fine," Billy said. He slid the brim around and around in his hands.

Rock narrowed his eyes. "You afraid, Slyboots?"

"Nope." Billy shifted from one foot to the other. He had no idea what to do. What if he failed? He didn't like the idea that Rock and Jackson would be watching him.

"You can't arrive in Nebraska City wearing that plug," Jackson said.

"Get going." Rock gave Billy a shove in the direction of a forlorn-looking young man leaning with both elbows on the rail, staring out at the river bluffs.

Billy took a deep breath. He gave his hat a quick dusting. "Hot weather," he said to the stranger.

"Yep." The stranger glanced at Billy for a moment, then studied the bluffs again.

Billy tried to calculate the size of the skinny man's head. The young man's hat was sweat-stained and dirty. *Might even have graybacks.* The thought of lice convinced Billy he didn't want the hat after all. As soon as he turned to walk away, however, he saw Jackson and Rock signaling to him to turn around and make a deal. Billy cleared his throat. He leaned against the railing, holding his hat in both hands. "Got this hat at a fancy store in Saint Joe," Billy said slowly. "Want to make a trade?"

"Nope."

Billy chewed his lip. He glanced at Jackson and Rock. They were still standing there watching him. It was clear Billy wasn't going to get away very easily. "Thirsty?" Billy asked in desperation.

"Yep."

"Give you a nickel for a soda water plus a trade of my fine hat for yours."

The stranger looked at him as if he were crazy from the heat. "For two dollars I'll consider it."

"Two dollars!" Billy said in exasperation. "That's twice what my hat cost brand new. And yours looks as old as Adam."

"Take it or leave it."

Billy sighed. He dug into the money bag and tried as discreetly as possible to give the stranger the money. The young man held the silver dollars up in the air to check if they were real, then he pocketed the coins. "Here's your trade." He handed over the battered hat and sauntered away with Billy's plug on his head.

"That was a sorry exchange!" Jackson exclaimed as soon as Billy returned with his new soft hat. "You weren't supposed to pay good cash money, Slyboots. You were supposed to make a trade. How we going to eat tonight?"

"He wasn't going to give it up," Billy said in a miserable voice. "What else was I supposed to do?"

"Better leave the haggling to us from now on," Rock said, and spit. "You ain't got the spine for it."

When the steamboat docked briefly at Brownville, Rock insisted that Billy hand over the money bag. "I'll find the best deal for our noonday grub," Rock promised.

While Rock went ashore, Billy and Jackson sat in the shade on deck. "Because I like you, Billy," Jackson said, "I have determined to give you my opinion of Rock."

Billy glanced with skepticism at Jackson, who was busy cleaning his teeth with an ivory toothpick.

"His bad qualities are chiefly an almost total want of delicacy or consideration for another's peculiar feelings, and a terrible large development of selfishness. His morality is of a very inferior quality, and only the question of expediency would prevent him, were the opportunity offered, from doing a great many things both unlawful and wrong."

Billy scratched his head. It seemed to him as if Jackson were describing himself. "He must have some good qualities."

"A love of home and relatives," Jackson said, poking between his front teeth. "A tolerable strong resolution, some energy, an affectionate temperament, a small quantity of pride."

"How come you're his friend?"

Jackson smiled and replaced the toothpick in a little case inside his coat pocket. "As a man, I do not like him. He being quick and impulsive, and I also, we are constantly agreeing to disagree. I assume we will keep this little conversation private and confidential?"

Billy nodded, although he felt confused. He was tired of keeping secrets.

When Rock returned, they ate a dozen stale crackers and a soggy pie made from dried apples, and drank a bottle of soda water. "Got everything for just thirty-five cents," Rock bragged. "A real bargain."

Jackson coughed delicately. "Thirty-five cents? I find that difficult to believe."

"You accusing me of being a liar?" Rock demanded.

"Certainly not, dear Rock. I only hope you didn't steal such questionable victuals."

Rock frowned. "So what if I did?"

Jackson shrugged. When Rock wasn't looking, Jackson gave Billy a knowing "I-told-you" glance.

It was nearly two thirty in the morning before the *Denver* arrived in Nebraska City. The town was dark and deserted except for a yowling pair of tomcats. Not a light shone in any of the stores on Main Street. "Well, boys, I suggest we try to catch a nap here," said Jackson, taking a seat on the boardwalk.

"Right here?" asked Billy. The only people he had ever seen asleep on the sidewalk back in Saint Joe were drunks and old homeless men. If someone he knew saw him dozing, sprawled on the ground, and told his mother, she'd be horrified. Billy smiled. He settled himself on the boardwalk.

"Ain't so bad once you forget where you is," said Rock, who leaned back against the peeling wall of a building.

# Chapter Three

BILLY TRIED TO SLEEP, BUT HIS STOMACH GROWLED TOO
ferociously. Whenever he closed his eyes, he kept imagining a
big dinner with a shank of beef and a mountain of potatoes
smothered in Ma's best brown gravy, with biscuits and a side of
her special yellow cake. As best he could, he arranged his
lumpy valise beneath his head, curled up in a ball, and
attempted to doze.

That night he had a terrible dream that he was stolen by
Gypsies. After Ma stole him back, he was kidnapped again.
"You're not my mother," he kept telling an old woman with a
wizened, dark face. "Can't you see? Leave me alone!"

The old Gypsy woman with jangling bracelets kept jabbing
him with a stick. "Running away from yourself," she cackled,
"is the hardest thing of all to do." She gave him another poke.

"Leave me alone!" Billy shouted, so loud this time that he
woke himself. Something hard prodded his back.

"You fellows best be on your way," said a deep voice.

Billy looked up and saw a man. Every time the stranger prodded Billy in the back with the hard, pointed toe of his boot, his spurs jangled. "We throw vagrants in jail," the man said. He towered over Billy with his arms akimbo. On each hip he wore a revolver. A silver badge was pinned to one of his striped suspenders.

"Yes, sir," said Billy, who scrambled to his feet. He shook awake Rock and Jackson. Jackson turned pale when he spied the sheriff.

"Haven't I seen you someplace before?" the sheriff demanded. "Where you from?"

"Us, sir? I can't imagine why, sir," Jackson said in a bright, confident voice. "My companions are from Ohio and Missouri. I hail from Vermont. We're on our way to Virginia City with Mr. Ed Owens's bullwhacking team, sir."

"Bullwhacking? Godamighty, Owens will hire anybody these days." The sheriff shook his head. "My advice to you greenhorns is to keep moving. Virginia City's more than a thousand miles from here."

"Yes, sir. We're on our way, sir," Jackson said, and tugged on the brim of his hat in a little bowing motion. Nervously Billy did the same.

"Shoulda told that foot licker where to take a flying leap," Rock said under his breath as they quickly gathered up their belongings. "Lawman!"

"What would that have done except land us promptly in jail?" Jackson scanned their new surroundings. He sniffed the air. His gaze seemed to settle on an unpainted frame building across the street. The large sign said CINCINNATI HOUSE. "This way, gentlemen, follow me."

The three of them headed through the door of the restaurant, a long, narrow room with a cast-iron cookstove at one end. The aroma of fried salt pork and onions filled the air. Eagerly Billy, Rock, and Jackson took seats at one of the half a dozen empty tables. A slatternly-looking woman wearing a stained apron carried a stack of greasy plates through a swinging doorway at the back of the room. Something made a loud splash, and a man's voice began to yammer in a language Billy could not understand.

Jackson whispered, "How much money do we have left?"

"Only twenty-five cents," Rock replied, "if you don't count the finder's fees we still owe."

"What?" Billy said angrily. "That's impossible."

"Had to use some to get a few bottles of tonic back in Brownville," Rock said in a defensive voice. "Wouldn't want me to get sick in the wilderness now, would you?"

Billy stared hopelessly at the wall where someone had printed the menu with a piece of chalk:

STAKE AND EGS WITH COFFEE AND SPUDS ONE DOLLAR.

NO CREDIT.

Billy's stomach growled. "You and your tonic!" he sputtered. "I'm so starved I could eat this table—oilcloth and all. Thanks to you we ain't got enough left to pay for one square meal."

Rock didn't reply. He simply smacked dead three flies that had landed on his curled fist.

"Watch yourself, Slyboots," Jackson murmured. "Paying for

a meal's a minor detail." When the waitress reappeared, Jackson removed his soft felt hat, ran his fingers through his wavy hair, and quickly twisted the ends of his handsome mustache. "Good morning, ma'am! Don't you look scintillating this fine day?"

The waitress shuffled closer in worn-out shoes. Her heels had long ago squashed flat the cheap backs. "What d'you want?" she said, and frowned.

"We shall have three of your delightful specials. Steak roasted tender, eggs lightly cooked in butter, please, fried potatoes, coffee, and a rasher of salt pork." Jackson smiled so tenderly at the unhappy-looking woman she blushed.

"Now, Jackson," Billy said anxiously, "we can't—" He stopped when he felt someone kick him hard under the table.

"And toast. Don't forget the toast, ma'am," Jackson said sweetly.

"Don't got no toast," she replied, and wiped her large, callused hands on her apron. She was scowling again. "That it?"

"I think that will be quite ample. Thank you so much." Jackson stroked his mustache. "Has anyone ever told you that you have a lovely profile?"

"Pro-file?" The woman's steely eyes narrowed. "You some kind of foreigner? Can't understand a word you're saying."

Jackson smiled, clearly undiscouraged. "Billy, you're a man of fine taste," he said. "Wouldn't you say she'd make a lovely sketch?"

Billy stared at the large mole on the waitress's chin and the dark circles under her pale gray eyes. Before he could say a word, someone kicked him hard under the table again. "Why, why, yes!" he said, rubbing his sore leg. "She's sure pretty as a painting."

"Would you do me the honor of allowing me to sketch your picture?" Jackson asked the waitress. He was already pulling from his pocket a piece of paper folded in half and a lead pencil stub. Elaborately he unfolded his fine silver penknife and sharpened the pencil.

"Nobody never made no picture of me," she said softly. She seemed so fascinated by Jackson's deft pencil outlines on the page that she did not notice more customers straggling inside the restaurant. A swarthy man with a bandanna around his neck stood at the stove. He banged pans and shouted what sounded like insults. "All right! I'm a-coming! Three specials. You got that?"

The cook smacked three pieces of meat into an enormous iron skillet. Rock drummed his thick fingers on the table. Billy's eyes darted back and forth from the waitress to the sizzling meat. How would they ever eat before they were caught? Jackson did not seem the least bit worried. He kept sketching away, even after the waitress had plunked down three mugs of hot coffee and three heaping plates of food.

"Can I see?" she demanded.

"Not quite yet, ma'am," Jackson said cheerfully. He covered the drawing with his handkerchief and began neatly and quickly to devour his breakfast. Rock lowered his head nearly to the table and used his knife to shovel into his mouth potatoes and meat and eggs as fast as he could. Billy gulped down his coffee so quickly he burned his tongue.

The crowd of hungry travelers grew. Nearly every diner appeared to be armed. A set of gleaming butcher knives hung on the wall by the stove, within easy reach of the foul-tempered cook. "You got a plan for getting out of here alive, Jackson?" Rock murmured.

"'O ye of little faith'!" Jackson said, patting his mustache with the corner of his dingy handkerchief. He made a few more quick additions, some shading, some more lines, to the pencil portrait. The smoky restaurant boomed with voices. Somehow Jackson seemed oblivious to the noise and the jostling as he worked.

Billy scraped the last bit of potato from his plate. "Don't look now," he murmured, and glanced toward the restaurant entrance. "Our old friend the sheriff's just arrived. He's waiting for an empty table, and he don't look happy."

"Hurry up, blast you," Rock said in a low voice to Jackson. "We got to skedaddle outta here."

"Don't we need to find that teamster outfit before they leave town?" Billy pleaded. Nothing seemed to make Jackson work any faster. He sketched away as if he had all the time in the world. From what Billy could tell, the picture didn't look one bit like the waitress. "Who is *that*?"

Jackson kept working. "Beautiful, isn't she?"

"Let's go, Jackson," Rock said. "We got less than thirty seconds to clear that door before they come after us."

"One moment, please!" Jackson replied. "Art cannot be rushed."

In spite of the crowd the waitress had not forgotten them. She wove past with a heavy pot of hot coffee. "You finished?"

Jackson nodded and with a flourish held up the sketch for her to see. Slowly she lowered the pot. Billy cringed, prepared for their ultimate fate: to be splashed with scorching coffee, threatened with guns and knives, then locked in jail for non-payment. To his amazement, though, the waitress's entire expression seemed to soften. She blinked hard and, with her one free hand, brushed away a greasy strand of hair from her face. "Can I keep it?"

"I would be honored," Jackson said. He reached into his empty pocket. "Now, how much do we owe you for this delicious meal?"

The cook hollered. Three nearby diners beat the table with their empty tin mugs. The door swung open again. "Nothing," she whispered, and snatched the drawing. She hid it inside her apron pocket.

Billy was on his feet at once, eager to escape. So was Rock. Jackson tipped his hat to the waitress and followed the other two past the sheriff and out the door as fast as a cracked egg slip-sliding across hot oil.

"Now, don't that beat all?" said Rock. He hoisted the trunk to his broad shoulder. "The likeness didn't look one bit like her. Not a bit. I'll never figure women. Never in a million years."

"My dear Rock," Jackson said, craning his neck to read the signs along Nebraska City's main street. "What is there to figure? One must simply appeal to their inner beauty."

"Inner beauty, in a rat's eye! Someday your crazy ideas are going to get us killed," Rock exclaimed. He darted around a lumber wagon. "Ever notice, Jackson, how every woman you sketch looks the same?"

Jackson leaped across a pile of manure. "Can I help it if all beautiful women look like Caddie?"

Billy tugged on Rock's elbow. "Who's Caddie?" he whispered.

"Don't ask, Slyboots," Rock warned. "Not unless you want that outfit to leave town without us. Hup two! Pick up the pace, you sorry soldiers. We wasted enough time this morning."

Billy stretched his long legs and gripped his valise in both arms. The last thing he wanted to do was miss the outfit heading for Montana Territory. Luckily they were able to locate Rosenblatt's Dry Goods, the place where they were to meet the wagon team boss, Ed Owens.

"You're the new bullwhackers?" Owens boomed. The wagon boss was a striking, tall, thin fellow with long blond hair that flowed over his shoulders. He wore an impressive wide-brimmed hat and leather leggings with long fringe. For once even Jackson seemed speechless. Standing before them was the most splendid Western plainsman Billy or the others had ever seen.

Without a doubt Ed Owens looked just the way Billy imagined his father. Bold and dangerous—the best shot, the best rider, the best cusser. He stood six feet four and was as tough as whang leather. He surely knew what to do in every emergency, just the same way Billy's father knew how to find the best claim and how to pan for gold. Even in the wilderness men like these understood how to survive on their own. They led rough-and-tumble lives, blameless and heroic. . . .

"Kicked the daylights out of him. One horn hit him in the ribs, and the other hit him in the side of the head and just shoved all the skin down off the side of his face in a bunch. You get what I'm saying?" Owens said, and stared at Billy. "This ain't gonna be no picnic."

Billy nodded, although he'd missed practically everything

Owens had shared. "Yes, sir." He shot a glance at Jackson and Rock, who appeared slack-jawed with worry.

"Where's the fees you owe?" Owens asked.

"Right here, sir," said Jackson, who took the bag from Rock and counted out the remaining $4.50. "And do you know when exactly we'll arrive in Virginia City, sir?"

"If I knew that," Owens said, and chuckled, "I'd be a fortune-teller, not a wagon boss. You got some kind of pressing rendezvous at trail's end?"

Rock's face turned red. "Ain't none of your—"

"We're eager to arrive, sir," Jackson interrupted. He smiled at Owens, but shot Rock a look of warning. "We're staking a gold claim, sir."

"Ain't every one of us? I'm gonna ramrod this train as fast and hard as it'll travel—or kill every one of you trying. We're racing snow in the mountains and Indians on the warpath. You get what I'm saying?"

"Yes, sir," Jackson said in a cheerful voice. "We won't disappoint you. We're excellent teamsters."

"We'll see," Owens replied doubtfully. "Fit yourselves out with supplies. Then meet me before sundown four miles west of town near the Spencer corral." He put his magnificent hat on his head and strode out the door.

"How we supposed to pay for supplies?" Rock asked the clerk. "We ain't been paid yet."

The clerk gave Rock and the others the once-over, as if they were as dull as shovel handles. "Mr. Owens foots the bill and retains the total from your pay at the end of the trip."

Billy grinned. He felt a wave of intense gratitude toward

Jackson and Rock. They were geniuses. Pure geniuses. Not only had they found Billy steady employment with a man who looked like a real leader, but they had made it possible for him to travel west in style, on credit. With delight Billy picked out a thick blanket, a rubber coat, a pair of good boots, a striped shirt, a pair of wool socks, a pair of pants, and a bag in which to carry them. "I'll need a gun, too," he said. Who would have thought he could own so many fine supplies for absolutely nothing?

"What kind of gun do you want?" the clerk demanded.

Not wishing to look ignorant, Billy searched up and down the crowded shelves. Jackson and Rock had already made their choices and were busy selecting bottles of whiskey. "What's a good one?" Billy asked.

"Colt revolver." The clerk placed a fine silver gun with a carved ivory handle on the counter.

Billy could barely breathe. He'd used a borrowed shotgun to hunt rabbits with his friends back in Saint Joe. Never in his life had he ever owned something as grown-up and deadly looking as a revolver. He picked it up. The gun seemed surprisingly heavy. This was just what he needed to go west across snowy mountain passes through dangerous Indian territory. "I'll take it," he told the clerk.

"What about bullets?"

"Of course," Billy said hurriedly. "Those too." When the clerk finished adding up his bill, Billy had spent $42.50 on his supplies. It seemed an enormous sum. "Are you sure that's right?"

"I'm sure," replied the clerk. His beady eyes glinted. "What's your names?"

Rock slammed his brand-new box of bullets on the counter. "Everybody got to ask so many questions in this backwater town?"

"Got to put your name in the ledger," the clerk said, and licked the end of his pencil stub. His tongue was as pink as a rat's. "You got a familiar voice, stranger. And I never forget a voice."

"We certainly don't know what you're talking about," Jackson said hurriedly. "His name's Rock Ruell and I'm Jackson Harcourt and this gentleman's Billy." He turned away from the clerk and winked at Billy. "What's your last name again?"

Billy nervously scanned the shelf with the canned oysters. Since he had a feeling neither Rock nor Jackson was giving his real name, why should he? "Chowder," he replied. "Billy Chowder."

"That's an odd moniker," the clerk said. "But I've heard worse." He scribbled something in the ledger. "You fellows should know that Owens don't take kindly to sharp dealers and swindlers who run out on him with his goods unpaid for. Unless, of course, you fellows enjoy spending time in jail."

"No, sir," Jackson said. "Thank you, sir."

Billy took a deep breath. He watched Rock and Jackson casually pack up their supplies. They did not seem the least bit worried about what they owed Owens. Why should he?

As soon as the three stepped outside into the bright afternoon and headed out of town toward the Spencer corral, Billy forgot about the debt to Owens and the possibility of going to jail. He forgot about the stolen money and his stepfather and the reason he had had to leave Saint Joe. He felt like a new person as he made the four-mile walk west of town.

In the distance he spied low hills covered with tender green shoots of grass. Beyond lay boundless prairie. Overhead arched limitless blue sky and racing clouds. Cool, bracing wind filled him with hope. Anything seemed possible. He bounded along, filled with joy and anticipation. At last he had crossed the divide that separated what had been from the great unknown ahead.

Rock huffed and puffed with their heavy trunk on his shoulder. "You surely are full of speed and spunk, Slyboots."

"Nothing against the law about feeling happy, is there?" Billy said, determined not to let Rock ruin his good mood.

Rock glared at him as he shifted the trunk to his other shoulder. "How come you're so all-fired to get to Virginia City?"

Billy nearly tumbled over his own feet. "What?"

"I think it's a reasonable question," Jackson agreed. "We have revealed to you why we're heading west. What made you pick Virginia City as the place you intend to seek your fortune?"

Billy hesitated. He knew how hard it was to lie to Jackson. *What harm's there in telling the truth?* "My father," he said finally.

Jackson looked puzzled. "Your father told you to go to Virginia City?"

Billy took a deep breath. "He lives there. I'm going to find him. I'm just curious about him. I reckon I just want to meet him, see what he's made of. That's all." He gulped, hoping his torrent of words would not reveal to Jackson what he was really thinking about his father. *He's going to rescue me and change my life.*

"He know you're coming?" Rock asked.

"No. Not really." Billy felt his whole face flush with shame.

"He's very busy. Can't be bothered with long letters. He's always working. He's a miner. Very successful. He's rich. But he wants me to come. He's waiting for me." Billy tried not to look at Rock and Jackson. He knew they were probably grinning. He had a sudden desire to give them both bloody noses. *They think there's something wrong with me.* In desperation Billy decided to change the subject. "So, Jackson, when are you going to show me the map?"

"The map?"

Billy shot a glance at Jackson, who seemed oddly ill at ease. *Good. Give him a taste of his own medicine.* "You know what I mean, Jackson," Billy said. "The gold-mining map."

Jackson coughed. "Oh, that! Soon enough. Let's get ourselves settled in first, shall we?"

"That's right. We got a ways to go yet. Plenty of time," said Rock, who began walking faster and faster.

"You haven't lost it, have you?" Billy asked with suspicion. What had Jackson told him about Rock? *"Doing a great many things both unlawful and wrong."* Maybe he shouldn't trust either of them.

"Not on your life," Jackson said and laughed. "It's perfectly safe. Come along now, bullwhackers. Our destiny awaits us."

The lowing of steers, the smell of wood smoke, and the laughter of men filled the air as Billy, Rock, and Jackson approached the camp. Fifty heavy wagons, with their tongues pointing away from the center, had been positioned in a circle. Sprawled in confusion among the wagons lay piles of supplies, crates, bales, and barrels. Beyond the camp in a pasture grazed three hundred long-horned Texas steers, an unruly, motley group of cattle of all colors with long, outlandishly curled horns. Billy soon learned that an ox was not a separate breed or species, but simply a castrated bull used for work. The oxen, most of them at least three or four years old, were often called bulls by Owens and the rest of the outfit.

"Quite a haul here. Looks like a couple hundred cases of whiskey. Couple thousand weight in bags of salt pork, flour, sugar, salt, coffee. Must be worth a fortune in Virginia City," said Rock. He tipped his hat to a hawk-nosed, spade-bearded fellow sitting on a wagon tongue cleaning his rifle. "I hear a miner will pay a dollar or more for a bottle of tangle-leg."

"Don't get any of your ideas," Jackson murmured. "This isn't the Union army, where nobody notices a ton or two of missing salt beef."

"You calling me unpatriotic?" Rock demanded.

"Not at all, my dear Rock," Jackson said quickly. "You know what I mean. There's a time and place for everything." Then he added in a cheerful voice, "Right this way, gentlemen."

Billy followed eagerly, swinging his new grown-up pur- chases over his shoulder. He stepped over piles of chains and wheels that lay about the camp. Here and there lounged nearly two dozen drivers. They were a mix of drifters, gripers, brawlers, drinkers, and occasional hard workers—the same kinds Billy had seen roaming Saint Joe in search of their next job, their next fight, their next spree, their next escape with wagon trains going west. Some wore the same simple shirts and grubby boots Billy had seen on farmers back home in Saint Joe. Others wore flashy kerchiefs, leather chaps, and spurs. A few were broad-backed roustabouts from riverboats. They tipped back flasks and sauntered among the oxen with superior looks. The bullwhackers with previous experience clustered in a group playing a rowdy card game. From what they were saying, Billy could tell they hailed from Pike County, Missouri—and they called one another Cousin. A few still sported Rebel caps.

Around the edges of the confusion wandered a beaky, pinch-faced fellow who introduced himself as Tosh. He told Billy and Jackson he was a Yankee jack-of-all-trades from Boston. "Anybody want to make some money on poker?" he asked Rock, and winked.

"No, thanks," Rock said.

"I'll be seeing you boys later." Jackson hoisted his supplies under his arm. "You keep your eye on Rock, will you, Slyboots? Make sure he doesn't get into any trouble."

"Sure," said Billy, wondering what Jackson meant.

"Better be back before grub," Rock called.

"Yes, Mother," Jackson replied, and vanished.

Rock and Billy left Tosh and passed a group of scowling roustabouts. "They're sizing you up, Slyboots," Rock said in a low voice.

"What do you mean?" Billy asked nervously. He could see that he was the youngest of all the bullwhackers.

"In the army raw recruits always got 'the inspection.' Same thing here, I suspect," Rock said. "Just don't act like a whiny, snot-nosed pip-squeak, and they'll leave you alone. And another thing. Never ask a man where he's from, what his real name is, and why he left the States. No bullwhacker likes to talk about such private matters."

Billy felt grateful for Rock's helpful advice. He was also glad that Jackson had insisted they get rid of their fancy hats. Who knew what the others would have done to them if they'd walked into camp in their city outfits?

"Hey, Tenderfoot!"

Billy paused to look around. One of the tough roustabouts laughed. Billy blushed.

"See what I mean, Slyboots?" Rock said through clenched teeth. "Don't act like you heard nothing. Don't give them that pleasure. Otherwise they're gonna torment you for the next one thousand miles."

"What am I supposed to do?" Billy asked.

"You're a big fellow. Act like it."

Billy grimaced. It was easy for Rock to say. He looked tough. He walked tough. He spoke tough. Billy had been in camp for only ten minutes, and somebody had already recognized him for what he was: a tenderfoot.

"Hey, Tosh!" Rock shouted. "Interested in a wager?"

Every man loitering nearby suddenly seemed alert. "What kind?" asked Tosh. He grinned and rubbed his hands together.

"A footrace," Rock said. "My man against yours."

"Nobody'll beat Slade." Tosh pointed to a lanky fellow with a red beard. "He's the fastest man in southwestern Pike County."

"My man's faster," Rock said, and clamped Billy on the shoulder.

Billy felt weak-kneed. He couldn't breathe. No words came from his mouth when he tried to protest.

"Ain't more than a lad," Tosh said, looking Billy over as if he were a game-legged racehorse. "Hardly seems fair. Slade's got a bad temper when he loses."

"Make the odds all the more interesting," Rock said. "What do you say?"

"I'm in," Tosh said. He and Rock began to hustle wagers from the other teamsters while the course was set up around the pasture. Billy and Slade would race eight times around, barefoot, back to the starting line—a piece of rope laid across the makeshift raceway.

"Ready?" Rock said to Billy. "Now, don't fail me. Remember what I said about the next thousand miles."

Billy gulped. He glanced at Slade's ropy, long arms and wiry legs. Slade stretched and kicked. He rested on his haunches and sprang up into the air to an alarming height.

"May the best man win," said Tosh, winking.

"That be me," Slade replied. He spit past Billy, then smiled. Since most of his teeth were missing, except two on the top and two on the bottom, Slade had a rabbitlike grin.

Billy simply nodded. His hands felt cold. His feet felt cold. He wondered if he'd be able to cajole his body out of fright into movement. He bent over and placed his right foot on the starting line.

"Slade! Slade!" the Pike County boys shouted.

Billy tried not to pay any attention. He wished he could hide in a hole and never come out again. Furiously he considered what Rock had done to him. *I'll kill him.* His face grew red. He took a deep breath.

"Ready? Get set."

*Bang!*

Someone fired a gun. Billy pushed away from the starting line. Slade shot past Billy. Billy dodged cattle manure and mud. He could feel his bare soles slap against the soft, slippery ground as he took the first turn. Slade ran several yards ahead. Slade's springy, confident step and enormous stride propelled him farther and farther ahead.

"Come on, Billy!" Rock howled. "Put some steam on! Remember what I said? One thousand miles!"

Billy shook off his feeling of failure as soon as he passed the group of howling teamsters. *One thousand miles. One thousand miles.* He kept repeating this to himself. His long legs propelled him faster and faster. With each bounding stride his arms stroked the air. By the sixth time he streaked around the pasture, sweat streamed down his face, his chest, and the back of his neck. His strides stretched, wider and wider. He no longer felt earthbound. He soared, aware only of the movement itself. He had become a hawk, flying free.

"Go, Billy! Go!" Rock shouted.

Billy did not hear him or the cheering crowd. Billy did not even count how many times he'd circled the pasture or how many times he'd passed Slade.

Someone stepped out into the raceway and waved a kerchief. "Hey, Billy!" Rock shouted. "You can stop. You won."

Billy slowed, stopped, then bent over. After having escaped the bounds of gravity, he was suddenly aware of intense heat. He could barely breathe. His chest heaved. Sucking in air, sweat streaming down his arms, he felt as if he'd just slammed into a brick wall.

"You won! You won!" Rock said, and slapped Billy on the

back. Rock was smiling as he collected his winnings. The Pike County boys did not look the least bit pleased that one of their fellow cousins had lost.

"Watch yourself, Yankee," Slade said to Billy. Sweat streamed down his bright cheeks and soaked his beard. "'Tain't funny to make me look a fool."

"Was a fair race," Billy insisted, then instantly regretted his words. He'd heard Tosh's warning about Slade's temper. Rock's idea to race had possibly made his life more miserable.

He had never considered that running could be so dangerous.

That evening Owens had a vast spread of food cooked for the outfit. The teamsters could eat as much as they could hold of roast pig, beans, fresh bread, and beer. Billy, keeping his distance from Slade and the others, ate until he felt he might burst. Owens strode with a bowlegged walk into the light of the campfire. His white hat and long hair gleamed. The pale fringe on his chaps danced. Billy wished that he had bought such a spectacular outfit, even though he knew that it would look odd on him.

"Listen up!" Owens shouted. He explained to the twenty-five drivers who was who. Each driver, Owens said, would be driving two wagons hitched together in a tandem arrangement. Six pairs—a total of twelve oxen—would be yoked together every morning before dawn. Every man reported to Owens and his assistant. In addition the wagon train had a night herder and a clerk.

Frank, who was assistant wagon boss, stood on a crate to be heard. He was a broad-faced young man with pale reddish eyebrows, freckles, and large ears. His oversize hat and crisp shirt looked store bought and untried. "I say, blokes," he shouted sternly in an English accent. "Expect bloody hard work from before sunup until after sundown."

The herders guffawed and slapped one another with hilarity.

"You hear, blokes?"

"Bloody hard work," said one.

"Where'd we find this foreign infant?" asked another. "Still wet behind his ears."

The more the men howled in glee, the louder Frank shouted. "We have an unfortunate late start for covering more than a thousand miles before snowfall in the mountains. As you gentlemen have heard, the Indian danger has become extreme. Nevertheless, we shall move fast and work like a team to outwit the savages." Frank kept talking as if determined not to give up. Billy felt sorry for him. Couldn't he hear the men howling?

"What gentlemen?" a teamster joked.

"Nevertheless, shall we?" another hooted.

Finally Owens stepped in by firing his revolver into the air. "Listen up. I'm foreman of this whole shebang. Don't expect no easy berth. You're going to work hard. But know this: Those who quit and owe me money, pay. Understood?"

The men nodded as if relieved that at last someone was speaking their language. Billy, however, did not feel the least bit comforted. He wished he had not been quite so extravagant in making so many tempting purchases.

"You want to pass muster with me, you do your job every day no matter what," Owens continued. For a moment Billy was sure he was looking right at him. He tried to remember what Rock had said. He pulled his shoulders back and tried to look at least nineteen years old.

A short while after Owens's talk the men started bedding down for the night. Billy crawled wearily beneath one of the two wagons that he had been assigned. Sleeping under the wagon was far more comfortable than sleeping on the hard boardwalk in Nebraska City. The grass was soft, and he had a fine, new blanket.

Lying in the darkness, Billy looked out at the bright stars that crowded the sky. He listened to the lowing of the distant herd. The ground thudded. He sensed feet stumbling through the grass near his wagon.

"He going to make it?" Jackson asked in a slurred voice.

"We'll see," Rock whispered, and hiccuped. "He's fast. Could be a good getaway . . . in a pinch."

Billy held very still and listened hard. He assumed the compliments were about him and his successful race. *A good getaway. That's me.* He felt proud. He hoped to hear Jackson say a few words of praise too. But he was disappointed. Jackson and Rock kept walking, wobbling through the grass, talking about things that didn't make any sense in the overheard snatches.

"Think he'll show?" Jackson asked.

"Keep your voice down," Rock replied. "Want the whole world to hear?"

". . . hundred thousand . . . can't miss."

". . . too late . . . river crossing."

". . . rich . . . find the place."

Billy finally gave up trying to eavesdrop. The two men's voices became fainter and fainter as they walked away. *Dang!*

Billy turned over on his other side and tried not to think about what lay ahead. One thousand miles. Snow and Indians. And now, a vengeful Slade.

Coyotes yowled. Billy reached inside the valise to make sure that the Colt revolver and picture were safe. Somehow he knew everything he was about to do would be worth it in the end. Making it to Virginia City and finding his father would solve everything, wouldn't it? Billy would be rich in no time—thanks to his father. Billy's life would be easy. When the people back home found out how wealthy he'd become, they'd admire him. Billy would be famous. No one would say, "Oh, Billy Crowley, that failure! It's too bad about him, really."

Instead they'd call him Mr. William Crowley. They'd name buildings in Saint Joe after him, and they'd invite him to be the master of ceremonies at the Fourth of July festivities. Maybe he'd set off spectacular fireworks. He'd give speeches at graduation and confirmation exercises. People would flock to hear him—even the teacher who'd treated him badly. She'd beg for his forgiveness. And just to show he didn't carry a grudge, he'd install a great marble fountain in the middle of Saint Joe, complete with copper-plated cherubims with devilish faces. The cherubims would carry pointed tridents spouting water and they'd ride fat dolphins with nervous faces that looked just like his teacher's. Then he'd give money to the poor to buy candy and mittens and the mayor would stop and remove his hat and bow when Billy passed him on the sidewalk and say, "How are you today, Mr. Crowley?"

Billy yawned. Maybe he'd have the fountain's cherubims riding elephants. He tried to imagine spouting elephants in wire-rimmed glasses, but in a few moments he was fast asleep.

# Chapter Four

———◆◆◆———

"ROLL OUT! ROLL OUT! THE BULLS ARE COMING!"

The ground trembled. Louder and stronger roared the rumbling, like thunder from an approaching storm. Billy stumbled in terror out from under his wagon. Half asleep, he was certain he was in the midst of an elephant stampede. Through the darkness burst an even worse nightmare. Three hundred half-wild long-horned Texas steers snorted and bellowed through an opening in the circle of wagons, rushing like a wall of water as they poured, shoulder to shoulder, into the center of the corral.

In desperation Billy leaped up into his loaded wagon, certain that at any moment he would be knocked flat and smashed to jelly beneath twelve hundred heavy hooves. "Yoke up!" Owens yelled to Billy and the others. Billy gulped and did not budge. The order seemed impossible.

Each towering ox weighed nearly one thousand pounds. The oxen tossed their deadly, twisted two-foot-long horns and slammed against one another. After months of roaming and grazing in open grasslands many of these wild creatures were not accustomed to being crowded into such a small, man-made space. They balked, stumbled sideways, and butted against one another and against the wagons with the powerful, uncontrolled fury of trapped beasts.

Standing atop a wagon wheel, waving his broad hat, Owens shouted assignments. "Slade, those two brindles are your leaders! Tosh, the blacks with white patches! Fitch, you take the belted brown and black!"

The experienced bullwhackers whistled shrilly. They shouted, swore, and darted fearlessly into the unruly herd with long wooden yokes balanced on one shoulder. Billy watched with a growing sense of dread. He had grown up where he never needed to know how to harness anything more unruly than the old dappled mare that pulled the hearse down Saint Joe's main street for funerals. He'd never milked a cow in his life. How was he supposed to yoke these stomping, half-crazed steers? How could he possibly remember which dozen oxen made up his team? He had no idea where to start.

Out of the milling mass of prodding, furious animals, each driver not only had to identify, round up, and yoke a dozen specific oxen, but had to do it in the proper order. The first pair in line, called the leaders, were the team's brains and set the pace. These oxen were followed by three pairs of unbroken riffraff known as the swing. Next in line were the slightly more experienced pair called the pointers, and last came the wheelers, the steady and reliable oxen that could be counted on in emergencies. The order and the exact position of the individuals in the pair had to be maintained. The nigh ox, as it was called, stood nearest the teamster, who was always supposed to walk on the left side of the team. The off ox was yoked beside the nigh ox.

"What you waiting for?" Owens bellowed to Billy. He pointed to a nearby wagon where one of the more experienced bullwhackers was struggling to control a stubborn pair temporarily tied to one of the wheels. "Yoke up your wheelers first!"

"Yes, sir," Billy said. Although overwhelmed and confused, he did not want to let Owens down. He hoisted to his shoulder a cumbersome, three-foot-long yoke, a slab of yellow birch slightly curved at each end.

The yoke was designed to fit atop the necks of two oxen standing side by side. To hold the yoke in place, each ox wore a U-shaped piece of wood called a bow under its neck. Billy had to get close enough to the ox to lay one end of the yoke atop its shaggy neck, slip the bow under its snout and neck, and insert the bow ends into two matching holes in the yoke. Then he somehow had to convince the animal to hold still long enough so that he could slip wooden pins through the bow to hold it in place.

The next step was to slip a chain through the iron ring that hung from the middle of the yoke. This stout chain, when fastened to the wagon tongue, was all that connected the team to the wagons, which weighed anywhere from seven thousand to eight thousand pounds each. There were no reins, no harnesses, nothing that tied the driver to the oxen. He was supposed to command the team by walking beside it, shouting commands, and brandishing a twelve-foot-long whip that Billy had no idea how to use.

Reluctantly Billy ventured into the swirling chaos of cursing men and thundering animals. In the dim light and choking dust every ox looked the same to him. Where were the two rust-and-white-colored oxen that he had been assigned as his wheelers?

"Watch out!" someone shouted.

A shaggy young steer wearing half of a yoke galloped past, swinging the yoke like a weapon. Billy dodged just in time as the ox slammed into a wagon, tearing the canvas covering.

"Gee! Haw!"

"Blasted son of the devil! Bull pizzle! Bucket of worthless guts!"

The massive off wheeler that Owens had assigned to Billy stood at the edge of the corral, calmly grazing in a teamster's hanging laundry. The ox dwarfed Billy, whose shoulders came barely to the beast's spine. One horn was curled backward, the other was broken at the tip. As Billy approached, the rust-and-white steer turned and looked at him with a sullen glare. Its black eyes shone like mirrors. The teeth in its enormous, slobbering mouth made ominous grinding sounds. Every so often its pink tongue, which was as big as a child's forearm, appeared and disappeared as it chewed a handkerchief and part of a shirt. "Hold steady. Please hold steady, now," Billy said in a low, encouraging voice, not sure what he was supposed to say or do. *Does it have a name?*

As best he could, he tried to copy a more experienced bullwhacker nearby. But the ox, as if sensing his inexperience and fear, wandered out of reach and began chewing a lost hat.

"Now, now. Be a good ox, will you?" Billy pleaded. He lifted the heavy yoke to place it on the creature's neck. The ox shook its big head. The yoke fell off. The ox wandered away again.

Billy picked up the yoke and followed the stubborn creature. Just as he was about to place the yoke on its neck again, the
ox turned its head and grazed Billy's forehead with the tip of its
jagged horn. Billy did not even notice; he was so intent on slipping the bow beneath its muddy neck.

"Come on, now! Dang you!" Billy shouted. The bow came
apart from the yoke four times before he finally got one end
fastened. The second bow pin slipped into the mud and was
trampled twice. Earnestly he fished another pin from his
pocket and attached it. Billy felt very satisfied that he had succeeded in yoking his first ox. Then the animal shook its head,
the pins slipped, the bow disengaged, and the yoke tumbled to
the ground.

He had to start all over again.

The wheeler's mate, the nigh ox, was more cooperative. The
matching rust-and-white steer had been accustomed to wearing
a yoke. It stood very still beside its yoke mate until the last possible moment—just as Billy was about to slip the bow under its
chin. Then the yoked off ox trotted off, swinging the yoke
crazily. Billy grabbed hold of the yoke, and the ox dragged him
into the fray. He was squeezed, nearly stepped on, and crushed
by the herd as the ox dodged left and right. Billy held on for
dear life. The ox came to an abrupt halt. Billy flew head over
heels and landed in a heap of manure.

Hatless, filthy, and furious, he stood up and ran after the
escaping ox. "Come back here, you devil!" he screamed.

The off ox was unimpressed. It trotted around the crowded
corral several times before returning only a few feet from its mate.

Out of breath, Billy struggled once more to slip the bow under the nigh wheeler's neck. Finally, after three attempts, he succeeded.

The next four yoke of oxen were even more wily, riotous, and stubborn. Billy clumsily flung a lariat over the neck of each of these wild steers. With help from Tosh and two other drivers Billy attempted to drag and terrorize the steers in order to convince them to walk toward Billy's lead wagon. When one furious ox tried to break free, Billy and the teamsters held tight to the rope, dug their heels into the ground, and were skied across the mud and manure. Each unruly ox was supposed to be paired with a more docile partner. Unfortunately, every beast was more evil-tempered than the last. One ox twisted out of the bow. Another broke a bow and stampeded in a rampage around the corral, knocking things right and left.

"Hold the horn!" Tosh shouted. "Hold the horn!"

Billy tried to jump and grab on to the steer's horn but was immediately tossed to the ground like a limp rag doll.

Not until noon did Billy, hungry and sore, finish yoking the last of his string, the leaders. "We get any food?" Billy asked Jackson, who was covered in dung. His team was only partially yoked. Rock was busy chasing his wheelers around the corral, threatening to smash them with a long board.

"No food until we travel ten miles," Jackson said wearily. "That's what Owens said."

"Ten miles!" Billy exclaimed, certain he'd starve to death by then. It had already taken him nearly eight hours to finish yoking. He still had to hitch the team. This meant convincing the string of five yoke into position ahead of the wheelers. "Ten miles," Billy muttered. He might as well be going to the moon.

"Over here! Here!" Billy shouted until he was hoarse. Catching, yoking, and hitching oxen was like trying to trap quicksilver. Just when he thought he had them under control, they would find some way to escape. Not knowing any commands, not knowing what to do, Billy simply pulled and tugged and tried to herd the yoked animals into place.

After an hour of this torture Owens finally showed Billy how to get the team lined up so that he could thread the chain through the iron ring hanging between each yoke. Billy was filled with gratitude.

"Let's go, now!" Owens ordered. He mounted his horse and rode beside Billy's leaders to try to get the team in place at the end of the line of wagons. It had taken Billy so long to finish he was the very last to set out, right behind Rock and Jackson.

Billy walked along on the left side of his leaders. Luckily, the pair seemed to know enough to follow Jackson's wagon ahead of them. Billy's driving was more like herding. When he wanted to turn the team, he hurried to one side, waved his arms, and shouted. When he wanted to turn the opposite direction, he made the same exhausting move. The wagon wove crazily left to right, right to left.

During one of the rare straight stretches without a catastrophe, Billy decided he could look back at his two wagons. For a moment he felt a sense of accomplishment seeing twelve oxen pulling the two wagons. His team was finally moving slowly in the right direction. It seemed like a kind of miracle. *Ten miles.* Surely he could handle that.

That's when Billy saw the hill. It rose ahead of them, long and steep.

The chains clanged and clinked as Billy worked his team uphill. The wagon wheels crunched into the sandy soil. Slowly Billy's oxen pulled the heavy load, passing both Rock and Jackson.

"See you on the way down!" Jackson called to him.

"See you in hell!" Rock growled.

At the top of the hill the wagons unaccountably crawled to a stop. Now what was happening?

"Whoa! Whoa!" Tosh and several of the other experienced drivers shouted. Some of them quickly climbed into the backs of their wagons, where they hauled out heavy chains. They attached these to the wagons' rear wheels.

Billy shouted to his team to stop too so that he could copy the others and lock the back wheels of both wagons with chains. At the brow of the hill his wheelers held back just as they were supposed to. However, the leaders and the rest of the team kept moving forward fearlessly. The more the wheelers tried to halt, the more the rest pulled.

"Whoa! Whoa!" Billy shouted in desperation.

In seconds Billy's team and wagons roared over the top of the hill and hurled down the steep descent. Behind them rattled and lurched the two overloaded wagons. "Whoa! Whoa!" Billy screamed, waving his arms as he ran beside the team. The oxen could not slow down or stop. The force of gravity and the fear of being crushed by fourteen thousand pounds of cargo seemed to have taken over. The wagons swerved and bounced and crashed along. Billy watched in horror as the dozen oxen, as if in slow motion, careened to the base of the hill.

Fortunately a broad space at the bottom prevented complete

catastrophe. Billy's leaders charged between two other wagons, threading the narrow gap. The oxen, now several hundred yards from the main road, finally stumbled slower and slower, then stopped, slathered with sweat and breathing with their great tongues hanging nearly to the ground. Billy, too, could only gulp for air. He bent forward, one hand on the wagon wheel, and felt his heart racing in his throat. Somehow the wagons and team had made it to the bottom without overturning, without colliding. Before Billy could feel relieved, however, he noticed the jeering Pike County boys.

"Hey, Yankee!" Slade shouted. "Road's over here!"

Billy wanted to slug Slade. But he couldn't. He was too humiliated. He couldn't bear the idea of failing as a bullwhacker. How else would he ever reach Virginia City? With every last ounce of energy Billy possessed, he waved, shoved, poked, and prodded his team forward to join the rest of the line as the wagons began moving again. Rock and Jackson brought up the rear.

"Hey!" Billy shouted to them.

Jackson lifted one hand in a half salute. He seemed too exhausted to speak. Neither he nor Rock looked a bit like the frisky dandies Billy had met on the bank of the Missouri River. *"Easiest job in the Union army,"* Rock had said. What did he know?

For the first time Billy realized the enormity of their undertaking as bullwhackers. Every day for the next thousand miles or more they were going to have to keep doing the very same thing. The idea was so exhausting and mind numbing Billy felt like falling to his knees, curling into a ball on the ground, and going to sleep for the rest of his life.

• • •

During the next week the wagon train covered barely thirteen miles a day as it crawled northwest along the Platte River road, a broad, beaten track trampled flat of any vegetation. Choking dust boiled and hovered over the road, kicked up by the wagon train and countless other horses and oxen teams heading west or east again. To avoid another team's dust, some drivers spread out, so that the traffic snaked through the table-level Platte River valley in five or six lanes.

As Billy and the others walked along beside their teams, they glimpsed the sandy edge of what appeared to be faraway dunes. "Looks like the Atlantic shoreline with no ocean!" declared Tosh, who came from Boston.

As an experienced overland teamster, Tosh wore a pair of glass and wire goggles to keep the thick dust from his eyes. The goggles made him look like a big-eyed insect. For the past seven days a steady westerly wind had been kicking up fine grit into their faces. Billy understood the value of Tosh's bizarre goggles. He wished he had a pair.

Billy looked at the empty, treeless landscape in wonder. He had never been so far away from home before in his life. Was this what the ocean looked like? In Saint Joe he had grown up with bluffs and shrubs, houses and shops. This desolate, dusty, wind-lashed place seemed overpowered by an enormous arc of sky that made him feel puny and vulnerable.

Although Owens claimed that the Platte River road was actually heading downhill, it appeared to Billy, Rock, Jackson, and the other new drivers that they were struggling uphill. The eerie horizon seemed to tilt away from them as they slogged through thick sand that sucked at men's feet, buried wagon rims, and tugged oxen hooves.

Every so often a wagon train or a stagecoach would pass them going east. The go-backs, as they were called, sent up more dust into the drivers' eyes and ears. Sometimes the go-backs shouted gleefully, "Only a hundred seventeen days to Virginia City!" Sometimes they called out warnings: "We seen the elephant, and he thrashed us good!"

The most discouraging sight for Billy was the go-backs who said nothing at all. These were often families—sometimes scrawny, scabby children and hollow-eyed women and men—who stared ahead as if they neither knew nor cared where they were headed.

As he trudged along, Billy, too, began to feel overwhelmed. Never before had he considered the number of people returning east. How many had given up and left places like Virginia City? What if his father was among them? Billy made a special point to scan the passing go-backs for a man with a high forehead, big ears, and deep-set eyes. The photo wasn't much to go on, of course. And soon he became downhearted. With each passing mile, each passing group of wagons, he realized the crazy enormity of his plan. *How will I recognize him?*

Parched and dry, Billy licked his lips until they cracked. He tied a kerchief over his mouth and nose so that he could breathe. There was no escape from the alkaline grit that stung his eyes. "Don't wash your face," warned Tosh, who claimed that a good layer of dirt acted as a kind of protection. With so little water for washing or drinking, the prospect of cleaning himself or slaking his insatiable thirst seemed more and more remote.

Billy had never worked so hard in his life. Laboring from sunup to sundown made him wonder why he had ever thought dusting and sweeping under coffins in his stepfather's store was such a despicable, difficult job.

"Hurry up, now, I say," Frank shouted to Billy. The assistant wagon boss was on a horse. He had tied a kerchief over his nose and face to keep away the dust.

Billy glared at Frank, riding along on a horse while he was trudging on foot. "Get up! Get up!" he bellowed to his team.

"Hey, Yank," Slade called. "What happened to your speed? You're holding up the line."

Billy staggered along faster. He was acutely aware of what the other teamsters thought of him as a driver. Even with practice it took Billy the longest to yoke his team. It took him the longest to hitch his team. Incompetence and cowardice were among the most despised qualities any bullwhacker could have. And he was certain that everyone noticed both in him.

"Bull chips! Bull chips!" The cry echoed through the camp that evening.

As the driver last to arrive, Billy had been assigned the unpopular job of gathering dried buffalo or ox manure in a gunnysack. In the flat, treeless expanse of the Platte valley there was little wood to be found. When perfectly dry, the bull chips made a good, steady fuel for a cook fire. When slightly wet, the bull chips refused to burn and smelled awful.

"Here," Billy said, and dumped his collection of dried manure beside the small fire. A pot of water mixed with coffee boiled beside another pan of simmering beans.

"Watch where you fling those chips, Slyboots," warned Rock, who poked a sizzling batch of rusty salt pork with a fork. In spite of his ravenous hunger, Billy had found that the fried, slightly tainted meat had a bad effect on his stomach. He couldn't yet eat it without feeling sick. The only food that he could keep down so far was bread cooked in a Dutch oven set in the hot ashes. This heavy kettle with a lid contained what Rock considered to be his masterpiece: a lump of dirty dough he had kneaded from flour, water, and a kind of crude baking soda. After cooking for an undetermined amount of time, the bread was ceremoniously dumped onto a filthy cloth, hacked to pieces with a knife, and distributed among Billy and the rest of the mess. The only way to eat Rock's famous lead-hard bread was to dip it in hot coffee.

"Delicious as usual," murmured Tosh as he gobbled down his share of beans. Nobody dared complain about Rock's awful cooking. The only thing worse than his bread was his temper. Since they'd left, he'd been in four fights and had nearly sliced off Tosh's left ear with a bowie knife. Any insult seemed enough to provoke Rock into fisticuffs.

Billy was too exhausted to cause any trouble that night. He got up and walked over to his wagon. Often he fell asleep almost as soon as his head touched the ground. Plagued by nightmares, he'd awaken feeling like he'd had no rest at all. Tonight was no exception.

"Gee! Haw!" he shouted in his dreams. Bulls twice the normal size trampled everywhere. Some had faces like his stepfather's. Around midnight he crawled from under his wagon in a sleep-walking trance. He grabbed a coil of rope from beneath Jackson's rig and yanked the rope as hard as he could.

"What the devil are you doing?" Jackson demanded, half asleep.

"I can't get my damned leaders' heads around!" Billy hollered.

The nightmare stopped only when Jackson tossed water in Billy's face. "Why'd you do that?" he sputtered angrily.

"You were sleepwalking," Jackson said, and yawned. "Can't a fellow get a decent night's rest around here?"

Humiliated, Billy crawled back to his wagon. There seemed no escape from the horrors of his new job, day or night.

# Chapter Five

————◆————

BILLY AWOKE THE NEXT MORNING, IN THE COOL DARKNESS before daybreak, to the sound of the first hidden meadowlark singing as if its heart would break. Billy lay beneath the loaded wagon and wondered how he would make it through another day. Exhaustion pressed against him like a great stone upon his chest. His legs and arms ached worse than if he'd run fifty miles. He longed to close his eyes and go back to sleep, and yet he knew at any moment Frank would shout for them to roll out.

Wearily he turned over onto his side, rested his head in his palm, and leaned on one elbow. He reached inside the valise and pulled out the photograph to give himself encouragement. It was still too dark out to see the face. He touched the ragged edges of the pieces of the picture. He'd tried his best to restore the photograph, but it had never come together the way he'd hoped. Under the circumstances, he'd been lucky to save this much, the only concrete proof of his father's existence.

When Billy recalled that afternoon in early June, the day he'd found the photograph, he sensed the same awful twisting deep inside his stomach. Like running a race too long, too hard, and suddenly realizing the fellow he thought he'd beaten was already at the finish line. Nothing could ever be the same again now that he'd been burdened with the trauma of truth, the trauma of secret. And yet Billy knew it was important to remember exactly how the discovery had happened. After he'd heard so many mixed-up rumors about his father's disappearance, it was essential for Billy to be able to tell himself the story of that day exactly as it had unfolded.

The afternoon began innocently enough. A warm spring wind bent branches of budding cottonwood. Billy and his mother and half brothers entered Auntie Louise's sour-smelling house on the bluff to inspect what belongings remained after she'd died. The run-down place with slanted floors, soiled carpets, and peeling wallpaper was to be sold. Although almost every bit of decent furniture had already been carted away, Ma insisted they pay a visit. She was always keen to find a bargain—better yet, something that might be possessed free of charge.

A distant, shunned relation, Auntie had always been avoided when she was alive. Now that she was dead, Ma seemed to think of Auntie as a kind of lesson. "You need to see what happens," Ma said to Billy, "when a person leads a poor, ungodly life."

Everyone in Saint Joe knew how Auntie had never joined a

church. She had no friends and few acquaintances. She was given to occasional wanderings, when she'd chuck rocks at the Methodist choirmaster's windows. Billy had admired her for this. If he could have, he would have broken the Methodist choirmaster's windows too. Some folks spoke of sending Auntie to the sanitarium, but nothing ever came of it because she always acted perfectly sane and quiet after her brief, infrequent spells. She never hurt anyone. The neighbors tolerated her as a reclusive, unbalanced spinster from a family that Ma liked to say had no good sense to begin with.

"I ain't related to her by blood, like you," Ma said, and looked at Billy as if he, too, were tainted. "She's your father's sister."

Billy wasn't particularly interested. While he was being cruelly trapped indoors with the belongings of a dead relative, his friends were probably having fun fishing in the river for bullheads. Even his half brothers seemed to be enjoying themselves. They were busy tormenting a cat in Auntie's parlor. Billy sighed and poked through the keepsakes heaped on Auntie's kitchen table. There wasn't much of value—just a crudely carved wooden box, a ring made from braided horsehair, a few yellowed letters tied together with a ribbon, a kind of ledger, and a small red leather-bound book.

Careless and bored, Billy opened the book and found a photograph inside. He tried to make sense of the picture while Ma argued with somebody about a rocking chair with a caned seat.

The man in the photograph had a strong chin with a kind of cleft in it. Around his neck hung heaps of exotic beads. Billy thought these might have been the kind Indians made.

Slantwise across his chest he wore a decorative leather sash with small white triangles that edged each side. Strangest of all was the hand resting heavily on the man's right shoulder. The hand looked as if it were perched there like a pet squirrel. The rest of the body was not visible because of the way the picture had been torn.

The other mystery was on the back of the photograph. In unfamiliar handwriting was written:

Hank, Virginia City, January '66
Hello Louise, from your fond brother

Billy showed the picture to his mother when she returned to the kitchen. "Who is this?"

"Where'd you get that?" she asked angrily.

Billy showed her the red book. He watched her thin lips turn into a hard line as she studied the picture and read the writing on the back. "Louise!" she hissed. She uttered her name as if it were a hurtful curse.

"Suppose you can keep it if you want," Billy said slowly. As far as he knew, it was bad luck to curse the dead in her own house.

Ma shook her head. Without another word she marched out of the kitchen and through the yard, filled with old bottles, broken furniture, rusty tin cans, and heaps of garbage ready to burn in a bonfire. Billy stumbled after her and watched in bewilderment as she tore the photo to pieces and threw the scraps into the heap being assembled for the next burning.

"Why'd you do that, Ma?" he demanded.

"Hell and flames, where he belongs."

"Who?"

"Your pa."

Billy was so shocked he couldn't think of anything to say. He felt as frozen to the spot as a runner doubled up with a cramp. In all his life he'd never seen one picture of his father. "Ma," he muttered, "Ma, where—"

"I ain't your ma," she said in a low voice. She spit the words out like chunks of bad fruit. "Your ma died when you was born. She was your pa's first wife. I took you and raised you as my own after we was married. A lot of good my charity did me. Your pa went west and left us poor as church mice."

Billy felt all the breath sucked out of him at once. She wasn't his mother. His real father might still be alive. The note on the back of the photograph had been written only five months prior.

"I gave you a name. I told everyone, including your stepfather, you was mine. You was always a burden to me. An ungrateful burden. Well, can't you speak? Y'stand there like a fence post. Can't you thank me?"

Billy felt as if he'd been walloped hard in the chest. "Why? Why'd you lie?"

"Too many questions otherwise. I'm respectable now." Her pinched face flushed, she stood with her thin arms crossed in front of herself and hugged her sharp elbows. "Nobody knows about the divorce. Nobody needs to know."

"But my father—"

"Your father's dead. That's enough, you hear me? I'll treat you as my son as long as you pretend you are my child. You must swear never to breathe a word of this. Swear upon your mother's grave."

Billy gulped, horrified. *Your mother's grave?*

"I swear," he mumbled.

From the house came the sound of yowling and the screams of the two boys. Instantly Ma turned on her heel and hurried inside. The back door slammed shut.

*She's not my mother. They're not my half brothers.* He stared at his open palms as if he'd just discovered he had hands. Slowly he curled and uncurled his long, slender fingers—the fingers that had not resembled anyone's he'd ever known. On the backs of his hands stood fine black hairs.

*Does he look like me?*

A breeze raced across the yard. The scraps at his feet tumbled.

"Billy, get in here and help me find something for bandages!"

"Yes, ma'am," Billy shouted. As quickly as he could, he grabbed pieces of torn photograph from the rubbish heap and chased the other remnants through the patchy grass. He stuffed everything he found into his pocket.

Late that evening, when everyone was asleep, he hid in the cellar and, by lantern light, reassembled the pieces like a puzzle. He poked each piece into a kind of order, following the ragged edges, so that they matched. Two eyes together, the place where the mouth should be, the shoulder. One hand and part of the arm. Slowly he restored the photograph.

His father's deep-creased face looked crooked—not exactly the way Billy remembered from the intact original. His eyes were not quite aligned perfectly, yet Billy could still sense a

marked fierceness in his father's gaze. He seemed to be a pis-
toled, grim figure ready to declare that he of all men lived and
breathed as a veritable Nimrod Wildfire. He was most certainly
tough hided. Although the photograph did not show them,
Billy was sure that his father's legs were slightly bowed from
so many days in the saddle. He was the quietest, most dangerous fellow in Montana Territory. The one whom no one could
buffalo. He was wily and independent, the kind of frontiers-
man who looked at clerks and coffin makers, like Billy's stepfather, with contempt.

Billy turned the pieces over and reassembled them again.
This time the jerky, hen-scratched writing on the back of the
photograph was difficult to read. He imagined how his father
had turned the picture and cradled it in one hand as he wrote
with careful pen. The picture was as close as Billy had ever
come to something he knew for certain his father had once
touched. Each word of the message seemed fraught with mean-
ing. Why had he chosen it? What had he hoped to reveal? Had
he known Billy would find and read this?

Hank, Virginia City, January '66
Hello Louise, from your fond brother

Hank. His father had a plain, honest name, Billy decided.
Far better than dour Harold or, worse yet, comical Harry. His
father had come straight to the point: "Hello Louise." He was
laconic, not boastful—a true, rugged plainsman like the ones in
the forbidden novels Billy liked to read. "Your fond brother." As
soon as Billy read these words, he felt pangs of jealousy mixed

with hope. Did his father's affection include his long-lost son as well? Why had he never thought to contact Billy with such a wondrous gift—a genuine photograph of himself?

The more Billy thought of it, the more certain he was that his father was still alive.

*But maybe he doesn't know* I'm *still alive.*

Billy used a pot of glue and pasted the pieces together on a sheet of stiff packing paper for safekeeping. He hunched over, barely daring to breathe as he pushed each sticky scrap into place. Every so often he wiped the glue from his fingers onto his pants. He swiped the smears with his shirt. What had once been a smooth surface, a recognizable shape, had become fractured like an image reflected in rippled water. *It's the best I can do.* Carefully he recopied the message on the back just as he remembered it:

> Hank, Virginia City, January '66
> Hello Louise, from your fond brother

Billy tucked the photograph inside a cigar box hidden beneath his mattress, where he prayed that Ma would never find it. By putting the picture together, he believed he might finally be whole and of a piece himself. He would understand who he was. But in the morning he still felt hollow. There were too many pieces missing. Too many questions. Too many whispers and rumors. The burden of the secret and the silence quickly became unbearable.

Every time Ma looked at Billy, she seemed to be accusing him of betrayal. She had once appeared so prideful and pious.

Now he knew this was all playacting. Her untarnished reputation meant everything to her. If anyone in Saint Joe found out that she'd been divorced, she'd be nothing.

One night while he was helping wash dishes, Billy told her he was leaving. At first she acted as if she had not heard him. She wiped a plate over and over again with a flour-sack towel. Every so often the air rang with a metallic clang. She cocked her head as if fascinated by the boastful cheering of her husband and sons playing horseshoes in the yard.

"I can't stay here any longer," Billy said quietly.

She narrowed her eyes and glared at him. He'd never noticed before how much the pale color or her eyes reminded him of dishwater. "Go to him, then," she said, "if you think your life will be any better."

Something hard and sharp smacked him on the cheek.

Billy felt shamed and angry at the same time. *She isn't my mother,* he told himself. Even so, weeks later he could still feel the hot sting of her slap on his face.

"Roll out! Roll out! Bulls coming!"

Billy crawled under his blanket. Perhaps if he kept perfectly still, no one would find him.

"Get up, you lazy blokes!" Frank yelled.

Billy sighed and pulled the blanket from his face. He could hear Jackson, Rock, and the others shouting and cursing in the darkness.

"Blokes, he says."

"Crazy Brit!"

"I'll show him where he can shove his blokes."

Billy took one last look at the photograph. Then he tucked it back in his valise with his other belongings. *If Rock and Jackson can stand it, so can I.* He grabbed his hat, slipped his muddy boots on his feet, and crawled from beneath the wagon to look once again for his stubborn off wheeler.

# Chapter Six

———◆◆◆———

BY MIDMORNING THE AIR WAS THICK WITH HEAT. THE SUN shone with such brightness that Billy and the others spied odd sights on the flat, dry plains. What looked in the distance like a dozen gunmen turned out to be only a flock of crows. A mile or more away horses appeared double their natural height and men seemed fifteen feet tall. Once, Billy was convinced that a beautiful stream bordered with trees lay ahead. Two hours later he discovered that the oasis had been nothing but a mirage.

When they finally reached the spot where they'd noon and unyoke the cattle, Frank announced that water rations would be cut. "I say, somebody's been taking more than their fair share," he complained. "We have precisely two more days before the river and barely a half a barrel left per wagon."

"I say," Tosh complained in a poor imitation of an English accent, "no blokes have been dipping into the dang water supply."

Frank, red faced but silent, inspected each wagon. He discovered water dripping on the ground in puddles.

"Blast it!" Owens said, and threw his hat on the ground. "Can I count on anybody? Who sold us these defect barrels?"

"You purchased them, remember sir?" Frank said. "I believe it was in Nebraska City."

"I didn't ask who bought them. I asked who *sold* them. Go and tell the men to grease up their oxen. We got a hot afternoon ahead."

"Yes, sir."

The men sniggered. There was nothing they liked better than to hear their superiors abused.

"Why grease?" Rock grumbled when he heard the order.

"How should I know?" Jackson replied irritably. "Perhaps it lends a certain decorative touch."

"Ever get bit by a green-headed horsefly? Will drive an ox to distraction," Slade said. "Better get to work, Yank."

Billy frowned but managed to keep his mouth shut. He and the others painted the snouts and necks of the oxen with axle grease and tar—the only provisions in plentiful supply. The oxen, filthy and miserable, stared at Billy as he rubbed their thick coats. Just as Slade had predicted, the horseflies' stings were as sharp and piercing as wasps'. The westerly wind cruised across the plains, picking up grit and dust, which stuck to the grease.

"Remind me not to take a job like this again, will you?" Jackson said. "I fear I'll never be clean or free of insect bites."

Billy nodded, glad that he'd covered his neck and face with

the grease. He couldn't remove his shirt without being covered with biting horseflies. The tormented oxen swished their tails and bellowed.

Secretly, he wondered if they would ever reach the end of the dry plains. The iron-flat land was sandy, rocky, with very few spears of grass. Beyond were projecting capes and bluff headlands. A tempting mirage beckoned in the distance. A sea lay constantly before their eyes, a dull, cool sky blue color. The smooth water looked as if it lay placid and welcoming. And yet every step they took, they never grew nearer.

At noon the sun was too fierce to go any farther, but there was no shade except for what could be found near clumps of sagebrush. Billy unyoked the oxen. He looked inside the wagon and discovered only a few cups of sudsy-tasting, alkaline water left in the barrel. He cupped his hand, brushed away a few dead insects, and took a sip.

"How much farther?" he asked Frank.

"Owens said we should be coming to the river soon." Frank wrung out his kerchief and retied it around his sunburned neck. His fine hat and shirt were dingy gray and stained.

"The river!" Slade said, and spat. "That's the biggest dang lie I ever heard."

"I'll thank you to shut up, you ignorant Piker," Frank said. Instantly he seemed to regret his words. Slade was upon him, holding him with a tight headlock. Slade's cousins pushed up their shirtsleeves and joined in punching the assistant wagon boss with great enthusiasm.

"Hold up, there!" Owens shouted, and snapped the bullwhip in the air. Reluctantly the Pike County boys released Frank. He slumped to the ground, battered and groaning. "Who started this fight?"

No one spoke. Frank, still on his hands and knees, feebly raised his hand. "I did, sir. I'm not sure if I can walk. I fear they may have broken a rib."

Billy watched Slade and the others glance away with barely concealed amusement. No one complained of injury—especially when it had been inflicted because of one's own foolishness. Clearly, calling Slade an ignorant Piker for no good reason was dangerous business. By being honest about his pain, Frank had only succeeded in making the men respect him less.

"Get up," Owens said gruffly.

"But I don't think I can by myself," Frank whined as if he might start crying any minute.

"Get up."

Billy slipped back to the shade under his wagon. He had seen enough. Having felt weak and hating his own weakness, Billy was impatient with the failings of others. Pity embarrassed him. He knew how it felt to be pitied. Frank's big show of pain and emotion made Billy uneasy. Frank was a grown man, wasn't he? Why didn't he act like one? In this new, harsh, dangerous life as a bullwhacker recklessness and callousness were qualities generally admired. Everyone was judged by the same raw standard. Billy knew he needed to remember this. Competence, courage, self-reliance—these were abilities taken for granted. *No one notices unless they're missing.*

As the line of wagons passed over the last stretch of sandy hills, Billy had his first view of the distant Platte River. On a map the

Platte appeared like the body of a sleeper whose two sprawled legs, the South Platte and the North Platte, seemed to have been flung carelessly across the plains. The North Platte angled northwest, the South Platte southwest.

Billy rubbed his eyes. Was the Platte River real? The swollen-looking river seemed wider and muddier than the Missouri. How would they ever cross?

As they trudged closer, they discovered that the limitless, table-level Platte River valley was actually only seven miles wide. The golden Platte River, which had seemed impassable, was in fact just one or two miles from bank to bank. Strangest of all, the river—a moving mass of pure sand—proved to be only inches deep in some places. The oxen didn't care. They sensed fresh water and tender green grass. They pulled hard toward the river bottom.

Exuberant, Rock threw his hat in the air and cheered. "Hallelujah! We're out of the desert!" For once Billy felt encouraged.

Suddenly through the dust roared a stagecoach pulled by six lathered horses. They were headed in the same direction. "Out of our way, scum!" screamed the driver, who sat atop the coach as proud as a brigadier general. In the blink of an eye the stage thundered past and vanished.

"What a sweet sight! Ain't no mud wagon, that's for sure," Rock said, licking his lips. "U.S. mail soon to be replaced with gold dust, and maybe nuggets, too."

"Holliday's Overland, I suspect," Jackson replied. "On the way to Fort Kearny. Then on to Virginia City. Should be there in a week, maybe two."

"Concord stagecoach—right on time," Rock said. "He'll have a good payload in leather pokes coming back, you can bet for sure. Salt Lake?"

"Maybe," Jackson replied. "More likely Denver."

"You fellows sure know a lot about stage routes," Billy said, smiling. He had always admired the boys he knew who could identify the Missouri steamboats by the tones of their whistles. These were the same boys who could rattle off each port and estimated landing time. The mastery of so much information seemed like some kind of gift.

"Ain't much," Rock said modestly.

Jackson coughed. "Just takes keen observation."

"For fellows just arrived from the East, you sure picked up a lot of travel information fast," Billy said. "I thought you were in the building business, Rock."

"Building?" Rock looked bewildered. Anxiously he glanced at Jackson as if to ask for help.

"He means, dear Rock, that you are interested in building a palatial house, remember?" Jackson said. "Each of us has his own dream of glory."

"I've never heard a person who knows so much about stage-coaches," said Billy. "Anybody might think you were a regular employee, Jackson. Why, I bet you even know the name of the driver."

Rock grinned. "I can tell you that. He's called—"

"Stop showboating, Rock!" Jackson interrupted. "It's unbecoming. We'd better catch up with the others, shouldn't we?"

For the next several days they followed the south side of the

Platte River. Billy and the others discussed how many miles until they reached Fort Kearny.

"We must be nearly there," Billy insisted.

"You boys talk like Kearny's our home port!" Tosh said, and laughed. "You got a lot to learn."

When they reached the army post, Billy and the others were discouraged to discover that the fort was officially considered only the *beginning* of the trail.

"Don't that beat all!" Rock complained as they unyoked their teams. "We ain't even started, and I'm nearly drummed out."

Fort Kearny was the crossroads of all emigrant movement east and west. Every month thousands of wagons passed through the fort, which consisted of crude, squat buildings made of dried adobe brick. A low fence hastily constructed from cut chunks of turf encircled the fort. A garrison of soldiers—mostly unshorn, unshaven, and in patched uniforms—lounged around a string of log huts. Small groups of half-starved Indians had also taken up residence around the fort. They appeared and disappeared depending on the season and the weather.

For the emigrants heading west Fort Kearny served as a kind of oasis—a place to buy overpriced supplies, have their wagons repaired, or mail letters back East. Though the squalid fort was nothing like downtown Saint Joe, Billy felt glad to see a flagpole, to spy a chimney, and to hear the familiar sounds of a blacksmith's hammer and anvil.

Billy and the others had been back in civilization only a few moments before they heard of a new, startling regulation. No wagon train of less than thirty wagons would be allowed to pass the post. "The Indians are said to be very troublesome," Owens announced to the freighters on the afternoon of their arrival. "There's talk of a general uprising."

Frank, noticeably subdued, spoke in a guarded voice. "During the last few days the soldiers say they've heard any quantity of rumors of the Indians' threatening to clean off the whole road in less than twenty days."

Billy and the others glanced at one another in nervous astonishment. Could this be true?

"Several men have been killed at different places between Kearny and Nebraska City," Owens said. "We've added carbines and muskets, but we need to move faster. Fifteen to eighteen miles a day if we can."

Billy gulped. People had been ambushed along the route they had just passed, yet he hadn't noticed anything unusual. The dangers of the passage west loomed much worse than he'd imagined. What if he was killed? No one in Saint Joe knew exactly where he was.

On the day before they were to leave Fort Kearny, Jackson told Billy that this would be his last chance for a long time to write a letter back to the States. Billy had no interest in writing a letter to anyone in Saint Joe. *What would I say?* "How about writing to Virginia City?" Billy asked.

"At the snail's rate we're traveling," Jackson said, "your letter should arrive weeks before we get there."

Billy borrowed a piece of paper from Jackson and sat on a barrel outside the sutler's busy store to write a hasty note. Nervously he licked the tip of his pencil. Just as he was about to write the first line, he had an awful thought. "If you were to write a letter to somebody," Billy asked Jackson, the most worldly person he knew, "but didn't have an address in Virginia City, where would you send it?"

Jackson, who was busy scribbling his fifth letter, looked up. "There's only one place that's used as the post office. That's the general store. Just put the person's name on your letter. The general store will hold the letter till the b'hoy arrives and claims it."

"He isn't a boy."

"B'hoy," Jackson said in a disdainful voice. "That's what they call a miner in Virginia City. I presume you're writing to your father to inform him of your arrival?"

Billy blushed. "Maybe."

"You think that's a good idea? What if he doesn't want to see you?"

"What do you mean?" Billy clenched his teeth.

"When's the last time you two were acquainted?" Jackson asked with a pitying smile.

Billy looked away. "When I was born, maybe. I don't know. He'll want to see me. I got a right to meet him, don't I?"

"I suppose."

Billy studied the blank sheet of paper. He could hardly hold the pencil, his hand was sweating so badly. He managed to write, "Dear Father," then smeared the words with his fist. He felt himself slipping away, becoming invisible. When his father received this letter, what would he say? What would he think? He'd hold this letter the same way he had once held Billy. Just like a baby—

"You finished?" Jackson demanded.

"Just a minute."

*Think!* Angrily he erased "Dear Father." *How can I call him that?* He kept thinking of what Ma had told him: *"Your pa went west and left us poor as church mice."* He deserted me. He deserted Ma, too.

"We've got to get back soon," Jackson said.

"All right!" Billy hunched his shoulders forward and wrote as fast as he could.

"Finished?" Jackson asked. He sealed the last of his thick stack of grubby envelopes. His once impeccable mustache now hung dirty and bedraggled on his dust-lined face. Jackson peered at his reflection in the small pane of glass in the store's window. "What a pitiful sight! It's a good thing Caddie can't see me now," Jackson said. "And you, Slyboots, your hair looks like quills upon the back of a fretted porcupine."

Billy didn't pay any attention to Jackson. He was deep in thought, rereading what he had struggled to scrawl so far in his letter:

Dear Mr. Hank Crowley:

    I deeply regret to inform you that your beloved sister Louise died this past spring after a sudden illness.

    I am your son, on my way to Virginia City. I am fifteen years old. My name is Billy.

    If you did keep me, what would you have called me?

Billy frowned. It sounded so unfriendly. What if he scared him off? "How do you spell *sincerely*?"

Without warning Jackson pulled the letter from Billy and

quickly scanned the page. "Your penmanship is abominable for a fifteen-year-old," he said, smiling.

"This is none of your business!" Billy grabbed the letter. If he had been older and less intimidated by Jackson, Billy would have smashed him flat.

"If you want to hear from your father prior to your arrival, tell him to send you a letter at Fort Laramie. That's about three hundred fifty miles west of here," Jackson replied with a smirk. "At the rate we're traveling, a horse could trot to Virginia City and halfway across the continent before we made it to the Rockies."

Billy concealed the letter with his bent arm and added a few more lines.

Please write to me at Fort Laramy.
Sincerely, your son,
Billy Crowley

Billy sighed as he reread the letter again.

"Don't be so downcast, Slyboots. I hope you're not having second thoughts about the trip."

Billy grimaced. "Not at all." He folded the letter with precise care.

"Boss says he wonders if you'll make it."

"Me?" Billy gulped. Of all the people in the wagon train he respected Owens the most. Billy longed for one word of approval, one word of praise, from Boss. So far Boss had seemed to act as if Billy barely existed.

"Of course I shouldn't tell you this, but I heard Boss say to

Frank that you were having an awful time keeping up with the others. Maybe you should turn back before we get into dangerous Indian country. You're slowing us down."

Billy winced. He'd never go back. Never.

"Well, I can detect your reluctance to follow good advice. You must realize, however, that we're easy targets walking beside fourteen thousand pounds of valuable, slow-moving freight."

The last thing Billy wanted was for somebody like Jackson to call him a quitter. He had to find his father. Besides, he had no money to get back. He had no money to pay Owens what he owed him. He was trapped. Jackson and Rock were trapped too.

"Foolish follows stubborn," Jackson said, making an irritating clucking noise with his tongue. "And we still have a long way to go."

Billy's eyes narrowed. "You'd like it if I gave up and turned back, wouldn't you? Then you'd have a bigger share of the stake in the gold mine."

"A minor detail!" Jackson replied, and chuckled. "I am only thinking of your best interests. I'd hate to see you scalped and riddled with arrows."

"I am not giving up," Billy said darkly. "I am sticking to the end so I get my share."

Jackson smiled.

Billy had seen that grin too many times not to know what it meant. Jackson did not believe him. "You said you'd show me the map," Billy demanded, hoping to deflect Jackson's scrutiny. "This is as good a moment as any to make good on your promise."

Jackson glanced over his shoulder. "It grieves me to think you don't trust me."

"That's right. I don't."

Jackson sighed. He thumbed through his letters as if the map might be found among the envelopes. "It's a funny thing," he said slowly, "how you can believe in something so strongly that you think it's true. And pretty soon you forget it isn't."

Billy curled his fists. "You and Rock took my money and lied to me. There never was a map, was there? Never was a claim, neither."

"I didn't do anything but give you hope," Jackson replied. "Same way I made that Nebraska City waitress believe she might look beautiful to somebody. Same way you want to make yourself believe your father's waiting for you with open arms."

Billy jumped up and grabbed the front of Jackson's shirt and twisted it hard in his fist. Then he slugged him twice in the stomach. Jackson's blue eyes bulged, and he bent over. His letters went flying into the mud and floated in the horse trough. Stunned, Jackson collapsed onto the ground. For once he was speechless.

With new resolve Billy marched into the sutler's store. He plunked his letter on the counter. "I want to send this to Virginia City," he said. "To Mr. Hank Crowley."

Ten mule-drawn wagons carrying mining equipment had joined the freight line so that Owens's outfit of twenty-five teams pulling double wagons was allowed to continue west. It soon became obvious, however, that the two wagon trains were ill matched. The mules moved much more quickly than the oxen. When they pulled into the lead, the oxen drivers complained about the other wagon line's cloud of dust. But it wasn't just extra dust that proved to be a problem. Five of Owens's drivers had vanished.

The missing teamsters were rumored to have seen a notice for wood cutters to chop railroad ties for the Union Pacific. They decided to leave Owens's outfit for better wages and easier work. As a result Billy and the others now had five extra wagons to drive. A nearly impossible situation.

Luckily when they passed Cottonwood Springs, Owens managed to hire three drifters who seemed eager to join up. Another mile west they came upon a lonely ranch—nothing more than a half-finished log hut with a sod roof. As the first of the wagons passed, Billy saw a stout man emerge from the hut. He waved a red bandanna with one hand, as if he was signaling them. Beside the man was a mangy, knee-high black-and-white dog that barked in a vicious manner. "Roo-rooroo-roo!"

Owens, who rode in the lead, hailed the stranger and motioned for Rock and the others to keep going around him. Billy, who had purposely remained at the end of the line to avoid Jackson, walked slower and slower so that he could hear what was being said between the wagon boss and the stranger. The dog stopped barking only when the man said something and gestured with his hand.

"Greetings!" the heavyset man called. He used the bright red kerchief to dab his drooping white mustache. Billy thought he looked old. Maybe forty or more. In spite of his age he seemed to have the spry movement of a younger man. "How do!" he declared, bounding closer. "That off wheeler of yours is badly lame."

"Yep," said Owens, "ever since Willow Island."

"You try boiling some tar and mixing it with a little grease? Works as a good poultice if you can open up the hoof a bit first. That fails, try wrapping its hoof in a boot of buffalo rawhide."

Owens took off his hat and scratched his head. "You sound like an experienced hand. You know much about driving a team?"

"I know a few things. I know that horses gratify our vanity. Oxen don't."

Owens chuckled. "You looking for work, by any chance?"

"Might be. Depends where you're headed."

"Virginia City. I'll give you thirty-five dollars a month if you sign on as a freighter with me."

"Fifty."

"Forty-five."

"Done. Just let me get my traps." The man called to his dog and disappeared into the dilapidated house. He emerged with a small sack and a carpetbag. As he left, he did not even bother to close the door.

"What's your name?" Owens asked.

"Frenchy."

Owens directed Frenchy to the wagons that needed a driver and galloped to the front of the line.

"Scoundrel!" Frenchy called, and whistled.

"Your dog went that way," Billy said, pointing. He could see the black-and-white dog leaping and cavorting around Rock, who walked up ahead. The dog licked Rock's hands with exuberance.

"Hey, old man!" Rock shouted angrily. "Get your dog away from me before I shoot it."

"Yes, sir," Frenchy said, smiling. He whistled loudly. "Come along, Scoundrel, this heartless, cantankerous fellow don't like friendly, intelligent animals."

The line of wagons set off again. It wasn't long before rumors quickly spread among the drivers that Frenchy had been hired for forty-five dollars a month—nearly twice their wages. "And he's a Hoosier to boot!" Rock said to the rest of the mess sitting around the campfire that evening. "Never trust nobody from Indiana."

The other teamsters looked glum. "Makes you kind of wonder, doesn't it?" said Jackson in a low voice. "How come this fellow was out there all by himself? No friends, no family."

"And how did he come into possession of traps that seem to belong to Uncle Sam?" Rock said. "I seen his clothing. All marked 'government issue.'"

"We need another driver, and he knows how to drive a team as good as Owens," Slade said.

Tosh nodded. "I never seen anybody yoke a team as fast as that fellow."

"Ain't fair," Rock grumbled. "We should strike to get the same wages." He stood up and stalked away from the fire.

"Now what's making him so angry?" Tosh asked, nodding his head toward Rock. "I thought he was in a blazing hurry to get to Virginia City. A strike ain't going to get us to the diggings any faster. That fellow ain't never happy unless he's got an itch to scratch."

"Don't pay him any mind, gentlemen," Jackson said, and chuckled. "With young, healthy, swift-footed drivers like Billy here, we should expect to arrive in good time." Jackson raised his tin cup of coffee as if he were making a dramatic toast. "To Billy. No hard feelings?"

"No hard feelings," Billy said, and lifted his cup. As he took a sip, he caught a glimpse of Rock gesturing with animation at Frenchy, who stood at the edge of the next mess's firelight.

# Chapter Seven

———◦•◦———

EVERY SIX MILES OR SO FOR THE NEXT SEVERAL DAYS THE line of wagons passed abandoned and burned-out ranches— all that remained after recent Indian attacks. The ranches were nothing more than small, windowless sod huts that had once served as a combination dwelling, stable, store, post office, and tavern. The crude buildings had been constructed with bricks of plowed dirt stacked one atop the other to make walls. Haphazard rubble of fallen stones and crumbled mortar revealed the places where chimneys had once stood. Most roofs, of cottonwood timber and layers of sod, had caved in, so that sunlight scoured the hard-packed dirt floors.

"Looks kind of sad and busted," Billy said to Jackson when they stopped at one place to use the well. The water was remarkably cool and pure. Billy wondered who it was who had taken the trouble to dig so deep.

Jackson kicked at a pile of smoky, charred timbers, all that was left of a crude corral fence. Inside the tumbledown house he and Billy found a rusty washbasin, an empty bottle of Drake's Plantation Bitters, a legless wooden stool, and an over-turned table made from wagon boards. Long gone were the shelves containing sale items such as jugs of liquor, canned fruit, knives, playing cards, saddlery, and goggles. The only thing adorning one wall was a hopeful scrap of yellowed news-paper with a recipe for lemon raisin pie.

"Whoever lived here," Jackson said, "must have been in a hurry to escape."

"Reminds me of the Grattan Massacre," said Frenchy, who stood in the doorway and surveyed the damage. Scoundrel darted between his legs and dug around in the garbage heaped in one corner. The dog snagged an old bone and trotted outside to enjoy his treasure. "Little Thunder and his band of warriors came through and burned the American Fur Company houses near Fort Laramie," Frenchy continued. "Killed twenty-eight enlisted men, stole all the mules, and murdered the Indian agents."

Billy gulped. They had scarcely seen one warrior on their journey. It was hard to imagine what he and the other teamsters could do to defend themselves.

"You were there, sir?" Jackson demanded.

"I was as close to the action as anyone could get. Emptied my two six-shooters and a rifle. Must have been close to one thousand braves that day, attacking from all sides at once." Barrel-bodied Frenchy stood with his stubby legs firmly planted, and twisted in a circular motion, dramatically gesturing with his fingers in order to demonstrate how he had shot more than twenty attacking Indians all by himself.

"You must have been a cyclone of bullets," Jackson said.

"I was a veritable one-man army," Frenchy agreed. "If it hadn't been for me, the hostile savages might have wiped out the entire fort."

Jackson snorted as if he did not believe a word.

"Never travel unarmed," Frenchy continued. "Better safe than sorry." He hitched up his pants beneath his large belly. "Now, you, young fellow, should take heed of what I say," he said to Jackson. "I seen how you ride the wagon tongue and falter farther and farther behind the rest. Any Indian worth his salt could pick you off in a minute with one well-placed shot."

Jackson scowled. His lazy ways were well known. He never walked when he could ride. "I hope, sir, that you are not impugning my honor," Jackson said in a haughty voice. "I'll have you know, sir, that I served in the Vermont Second Brigade, and I am an excellent rifleman with nearly two years of active service to my credit."

"He and Rock drove wagons," Billy added, hoping to be helpful. He was surprised when Frenchy burst into raucous laughter.

"I suppose you can show us some helpful supply line maneuvers!" Frenchy said.

Jackson glared, mumbled a few curse words under his breath, and stomped away.

"Now, what do you suppose made him so upset?" Billy asked.

"Old war wounds, maybe," Frenchy said, and winked.

Billy and Frenchy went outside and sat on overturned barrels in the shade. Scoundrel placed his long snout on Billy's knee. The dog seemed to study Billy with great care. Scoundrel's bright, dark eyes examined Billy so intently he had no choice but to scratch the dog's head. "Some fine animal," Billy said.

"Wouldn't know to look at him what a sorry life this stray had," Frenchy said. "Found him abandoned, lame, and half starved on the road to Virginia City. Plumped up and recovered fine. Best dog I ever had. Aren't you, Scoundrel?"

The dog pricked up his ears when he heard his name. As soon as Billy stopped scratching the dog's head, Scoundrel pawed his leg. "He knows what he wants," Billy said, chuckling. He patted the dog again.

"Scoundrel's a bold one. A tireless herder, excellent hunter, renowned watchdog, and loyal companion."

"Why would someone abandon such a remarkable creature?"

Frenchy shrugged. "Can't say. Even if Scoundrel could talk, I doubt he could tell us the whole story."

"What do you mean?"

"He only knows what happened to him. He probably doesn't understand why. There could have been all kinds of reasons mixed up together. Poverty, loneliness, pride, anger, ignorance. Maybe even love."

"Love?" Billy frowned. "That doesn't make sense."

"Maybe some folks loved him so much they thought the best thing for him was to find a new owner. Maybe they just couldn't take care of him. They simply hoped for the best and set him free."

"Doesn't sound like love to me. Scoundrel nearly died for want of care till you came along and rescued him."

"Sometimes I think he rescued me," Frenchy said. "You see, I intend to go to Montana, make my fortune, and set myself up with a fine spread. A ranch with a couple thousand acres. I figure I'll raise cattle. Scoundrel's going to be my right hand. What about you? Why are you heading west?"

Billy told Frenchy how he'd left Saint Joe to find his father in Virginia City. "He's the only one who can tell me about himself. He can tell me about my mother, too. She died when I was born."

Frenchy nodded. "Makes sense to find out where you came from. Only way you can know how you fit."

"You don't think it's a crazy idea?"

"Not at all."

Billy hunched his shoulders forward and stared at the ground as he dug the toe of his boot into the dirt. "I have some other ideas too," he said in a low voice. "How my pa's going to teach me how to wrest gold from the ground. We're going to be partners in a quartz claim. We'll work together. He's a knowledgeable, respected miner." He looked up to study Frenchy's face.

Frenchy nodded as if he was listening carefully. "It's a good thing to have somebody show you how to twist the drill and hold it steady while the doublejack swings past your head. You'll need to learn how to make the color show by shaking the Long Tom and how to tamp black powder carefully into deep-drilled holes in solid rock and how to use dynamite. An experienced miner will know the value of each claim in the gulch as well as the name of the assayer."

Billy bit his lower lip. There seemed to be a great deal more to prospecting than he'd considered. "Were you ever a miner?"

Frenchy chuckled. "I can tell the difference between a piece of quartz and a chunk of sandstone without any trouble. Maybe you and your pa can prospect for gold outcroppings in the hills the way other sons and fathers search for good fishing holes."

Billy smiled. He liked the sound of that. Encouraged, he told Frenchy other plans that he'd never shared with anyone. How he hoped that he and his father would work together side by side and then share beans over the fire at the end of the day. Neither of them would have to talk because they'd each know what the other was thinking. "I'll respect him and he'll respect me," Billy said. "In the gold camp everyone will know us. It'll be 'Crowley and his son' this and 'Crowley and his son' that. I'll be one of the b'hoys, and my father'll be proud and say so."

"Admirable aspirations." Frenchy rose to his feet. "I hope you find what you're looking for."

Scoundrel jumped up and licked Billy in the face. Billy laughed, surprised by how joyful he suddenly felt. Maybe everything would work out after all.

"Yoke up! Yoke up!" Frank shouted. "Watch for Indians!"

When they drove away after hitching the oxen, Billy and the other drivers kept careful watch along the sandy ridges and low, brushy places for any sign of skulking warriors. They narrowed the gaps between wagons and kept loaded guns within easy reach. In spite of these precautions every screaming cry of a hawk seemed to Billy to be the sound of Indians signaling to one another. When he spied sudden movement on the horizon, he assumed it was a group of Indian scouts—not the darting stampede of a pronghorn herd.

That evening they camped near an alkali lake, where Billy and Rock and several others from their mess washed out their dirty, stinking shirts for the first time since they'd left Saint Joe. Washing laundry was a tedious job, since they had only a sliver of lye soap between them. Billy rubbed the ragged shirt on a rock, smacked it in the water, twisted it hard, and dipped it in the water again. "Doesn't look any better," Billy said, and held the shirt to his face. "Or smell much better either."

Scoundrel seemed fascinated by the operation and kept sniffing around Rock. "Get away from me, you mangy foot licker!" he warned.

Billy laughed. "He seems to like you."

Rock scowled. He picked up a stone and tossed it at the dog. Scoundrel ran yelping back to camp.

"Didn't need to do that, Rock," Billy complained. "What did that dog ever do to you?"

"Mind your own business, Slyboots, if you know what's good for you." Rock twisted his wet shirt until his muscles showed. "Now what's that old fool up to?" He stared from the edge of the lake to the place where they had built a cooking fire.

Frenchy tapped a tin cup with a knife and called, "Chow time! Chow time!"

The others in their mess were already gathered eagerly

around the fire, awaiting to share Frenchy's concoction—a shortbread made with his own private store of sweet raisins and sugar. Frenchy broke off chunks of the browned biscuit for every man in the mess.

"You can even bite into it without losing your teeth!" Tosh declared in admiration. "You should take some cooking lessons from Frenchy, Rock."

Everyone around the fire laughed nervously. Rock scowled. His bread was so hard that the men joked it should be wedged beneath wheels to keep their wagons from rolling down hills.

"Drink up!" Frenchy said, beaming with pleasure. He passed around his own private jug.

"Here's to Frenchy!" Slade said, raising his cup with enthusiasm. Everyone except Rock echoed this toast. He lifted his cup briefly, then tossed back Frenchy's special home brew.

Billy sputtered and coughed when he tried to swallow. The strong liquid set his throat on fire. "Whoa, partner!" Frenchy said, and slapped him on the back. "Go easy, now, on that painkiller."

Slade took a sip. "Strong enough to cure snakebite," he said, eyes bulging. "There's right smart of rattlesnakes around here."

Billy glanced anxiously into the growing shadows. He'd seen a few brown sidewinders slithering under sagebrush that afternoon. He'd made it a habit every night before he went to sleep under the wagon to check his blanket for any scaly invaders.

Frenchy passed around the jug again. Everyone obliged by refilling their cups. "Have you killed rattlesnakes with your bare hands, Frenchy?" demanded Jackson with a mocking grin.

Frenchy paused for a moment and swirled his whiskey in his cup. "I have always believed, gentlemen, that if you gain the affection of a rattlesnake through some special act of kindness, the serpent may later thank you for your efforts."

The men laughed uproariously. Jackson and Rock exchanged disgusted glances.

"Hear me out!" Frenchy said, holding one hand in the air. His dog circled once, twice, and settled comfortably at his master's feet in a warm place by the fire. "Once upon a time I found a six-foot rattler trapped under a boulder that had rolled upon it while it was relaxing in the sun. Now, I could have blown the snake's brains out of its head without another thought. But I did not. Instead I freed the poor creature. In gratitude thereafter this snake followed me wherever it was permitted to go and guarded me faithfully."

"A likely story!" Rock said, and took another long swallow. "Next you'll tell us you named that dang snake."

"I most certainly did," Frenchy replied in all seriousness. "In honor of my home state of Indiana I called that rattlesnake Annie."

"Annie?" Billy asked.

"From the name Indi-*anna*, my friend," Frenchy said, and smiled. "One night on being awakened, I noticed that Annie was missing from the place where she usually slept inside the sod wall. So I jumped up and went to see what happened. I lit a candle, opened the door, and heard her a-rattling her tail as loud as a snare drum. Well, imagine my surprise when I discovered that the snake had run a skulking Indian into the other room. She was holding him there a prisoner while her tail stuck out the window, rattling like a cavalry charge, calling me to come in and help kill the cuss!"

The men hooted with approval. For a third time the jug was passed around the circle. "How," declared Jackson, wobbling to his feet, "do we know you're not lying?"

Frenchy grinned with satisfaction. Scoundrel, who had been lying peacefully at his feet all this time, thumped his tail against the ground. "I have lived in the West nearly all my life," he declared, "and I have never yet been lynched. This, my friends, is irrefutable proof of my good moral character."

Everyone except Rock and Jackson cheered. Only Jackson and Rock seemed unmoved by Frenchy's generosity or his wit. Later Frank entertained them with a sad ballad. Tosh played the harmonica and Sweeney told several tales of his adventures in the Confederate army. This was followed by several dozen exploits Frenchy had experienced in the Wilderness, Chancellorsville, and numerous other valiant battles. In every single one Frenchy was the bravest, most daring soldier.

By the time they emptied the jug, wolves had begun to howl in the darkness. Thanks to Frenchy, this was the most entertaining and enjoyable evening Billy had experienced so far on the journey.

"You fellows have a river to cross tomorrow," Owens announced when he finally appeared in the firelight. "Time to hit the hay."

The men staggered to their feet and shuffled back to their wagons. Billy, half asleep, stood up and patted Scoundrel on the head. "Good night, Frenchy," he said when they were the only ones left beside the fire.

"Good night to you, young man," Frenchy replied. Dying firelight danced on his flushed face. "What splendid, unfulfilled promise does every man make to himself when he is young and fails to keep in his old age?"

Billy shrugged. He had no idea what Frenchy was talking about. He was tired and knew tomorrow would be another long day. "Don't rightly know, sir," Billy said. "But thank you for your fine shortbread. Best thing I ate since I left home."

"It was my pleasure," Frenchy replied, all seriousness gone. "Good night."

As he wandered back to his wagon, Billy took one last look at Frenchy. He sat staring into the fire with only his dog for company.

# Chapter Eight

—◆—

THE NEXT DAY DAWNED WITH THE DREADED, EARSPLITTING cry. "Bulls a-coming! Bulls a-coming! Roll out! Roll out!"

Billy and the others who had enjoyed Frenchy's jug the night before could hardly hold their heads up or walk in a straight line. Frenchy's brew had more of a kick than any of them had imagined. They fumbled with the oxbows and cursed more hopelessly than usual.

When the freight line finally managed to get under way, they beheld at late morning the great, treacherous half-mile expanse of the South Platte. The muddy, brawling river looked surprisingly swollen for late July. The broad current buckled under willow stands and scrubbed a dirty foam from cotton-wood roots. In some places the surface bubbled like a pot of beans.

Although Indians had burned the small settlement of nearby Julesburg to the ground the previous year, a few stragglers had returned to rebuild. It appeared that they found it more profitable to offer high-priced help to stranded teams of crossing emigrants than to operate their previous businesses running livestock.

"Need a hand?" a local teamster yelled to a mule driver whose wagon was quickly being sucked under by quicksand beneath the river.

"How much?" the driver cried desperately as his wooden crates of precious cargo began to float away.

"Fifty dollars."

"That's robbery!" the driver shouted.

The Julesburg man showed no anger at this insult. He simply waited patiently as the mule driver lashed his poor struggling team. When two mules floundered, tangled in their own harnesses, and drowned, the driver turned again to the Julesburg teamster. "Help me, man!" he cried. "How much?"

"One hundred dollars," the Julesburg teamster replied.

At this point the mule driver was about to lose his entire cargo and agreed to the high rate.

As Billy and the others stood beside the swift-moving river, several of the men in the outfit grumbled quietly about abandoning their jobs and going on to Denver. Talk of desertion was silenced when Owens appeared. "The river bottom's quicksand and gravel. It's going to be hard pulling," Owens announced. "The only way to cross with oxen is to uncouple the wagons. We'll cross twelve oxen to one single wagon."

"Will take us from here to next Sunday to get over," complained Rock.

"That is, *if* we get over," Jackson added.

Billy tried not to feel worried about crossing with such a heavily loaded wagon in muddy water with a fast current. Although he had grown up along the Missouri and was an excellent swimmer, he knew that big rivers had moods and appetites. There was something very unforgiving about the way that a river treated fools. Like the others, Billy stowed his boots, valise, and pants inside his second wagon, where he would retrieve them later. From the looks of the others who had plunged their teams into the river, they all were going to get very wet.

"Yaw-ho! Whoa, haw!"

Bullwhips cracked. Men cursed. Water splashed. Oxen bellowed.

"You mean to say we have to cross this abominable river in only our shirts?" Jackson demanded as Owens led the first team to the water's edge. He had removed the saddle of his horse as well as his own fine leather chaps and boots. "This seems most extraordinary."

"A horse will sink up to its neck in that current," said Frenchy, who seemed to be the only one in the outfit the least bit enthusiastic about the crossing. "An ox will float higher in the water. That's why we ride the lead beasts over. Kind of keep them down as low as possible in the water so they won't lose their footing."

"Shouldn't be too hard for a man of your girth," Jackson said to Frenchy.

"My pounds have made me an excellent pilot," Frenchy replied good-naturedly. "Just remember to direct your team somewhat upstream. That way you'll correct the drift from the current."

Billy stared anxiously at the deepest place in the river, where the water swirled in evil, undulating swells. He knew that a river like this changed every day. A sandbar in a particular place one day might vanish the next.

"It don't look safe," Tosh said in a low voice.

"Yoke up!" shouted Owens when he had managed to swim his horse back across to guide the next team.

"Bet you can't make it, Yank," Slade said to Billy loud enough for everyone to hear. "Bet you get halfway and turn tail."

"I'll get across," Billy said in a steely voice. He could not bear for the other drivers to think he was a coward. Deep down he knew he was going eye to eye with the thing he had avoided: possible failure.

"Who's next?" Owens called.

"I'll go," Frenchy volunteered. Although he had inherited the worst oxen team, he had patiently managed to train them into a hardworking operation. "Come, boooooooossss! Come, booooooosss!" Buck and Tom, his leaders, came trotting over. In less than sixteen minutes he had yoked all twelve oxen and hitched them to the wagon.

Expertly Frenchy raised the cumbersome whip in the air and, using both hands, snapped it over the animals' heads.

*Crack!*

The sound was as loud as a pistol shot. "Get up! Get up!" Frenchy shouted. Unlike the other drivers, he never allowed the sharp, ragged end of the leather to bite the oxen's backs. The sound, he said, was enough to jolt the oxen into behaving. "There's no need," he always said, "to maim the poor crea- tures."

"You want to leave the dog?" Owens shouted as Frenchy's team leaned into their yokes and waded into the water. Scoundrel perched in the wagon.

"Never left him before. The dog stays with me," Frenchy said. "I will insult his honor if he's left behind."

"Suit yourself," said Owens.

Rock, Billy, and three other men were ordered by Owens to stand by to whip or cudgel Frenchy's team toward the water if the oxen showed any resistance. "Whoa!" Frenchy called. He waded into the waist-deep water and clumsily climbed atop Buck's broad back. Buck seemed disturbed and backed slightly, causing the other oxen to panic, until Frenchy shouted, "Get up!" Slowly the team moved deeper into the water.

"You want for us to give them a good lashing?" Rock shouted, brandishing a whip.

"You do, fool, and I'll whip you to within every inch of your life," Frenchy hollered back.

The lead team plunged up to their necks. Frenchy cried, "Easy! Easy now!" Using his voice and the sound of the whip, he managed to coax his team into the water and across the river. Billy and the others watched closely as Frenchy's wagon was caught briefly midway in the current but managed to make it to the other side.

When it was Billy's turn, he climbed atop his nigh lead ox's back and shouted at the top of his lungs to order his team into the water. The team refused to budge. They lunged to the right and the left to avoid entering the river. Finally Owens brandished a whip and forced the team into the water.

The ox Billy was riding sank deeper and deeper as he moved forward. Cold water swirled around Billy's legs. He sensed a thudding motion as the ox's hooves hit the river's sandy bottom. Inch by inch the team made headway across the river. With all his concentration he tried to keep the team pointed toward the opposite shore. At the deepest point midstream the team floundered because it could not sense solid ground.

"Come along!" Owens shouted from his horse. He waved his hat. "Keep 'er moving!"

The growing panic of the lead ox shot down the line like a kind of telegraphed current. The oxen bellowed and snorted, and for one awful moment Billy had visions of the team swimming and turning backward again, bent as they were now in a kind of letter C in the current. Any moment the chains would tangle.

"What's the matter with you!" Owens hollered. "Bring them around! Keep upstream!"

Billy hardly knew where he was headed, he felt so panicked. He smacked his ox on the side of its neck and kicked it with his legs, even though he knew that was pointless. Everything seemed to be flowing swiftly past his eyes—loose crates, logs, boards, spindrift, a riderless mule, driftwood. He glimpsed the bloated carcass of a deer, its antlers tangled with vines. The corpse sped past with cloudy, staring eyes. Without a fixed object nearby to concentrate upon, Billy felt as if he were being swept away by garbage and flotsam. The river was too wide, too impossible. *What if I'm stuck midway forever?* The oxen bellowed, tossed their heads, and churned the water.

What would his father think if he saw him at this moment, losing control so completely?

"Keep 'er going!" shouted Frenchy. He had mounted an extra horse and ridden out to Billy and his team. The very sound of the whip seemed to startle the team into obedience. With Owens and Frenchy on either side, the team moved forward again toward the shore. Billy glanced backward. The line straightened out, and the heavy wagon still appeared upright.

As soon as he redirected his gaze toward the goal—the opposite shore—the oxen stopped drifting, touched bottom, and began pulling again. At this point the heavy wagon had reached the middle of the deep channel. Billy felt a strange rumble. When he turned he saw the wagon begin to sink.

"It's going over!" Owens shouted, and swore.

The wagon tilted, then righted itself. "Keep 'er moving!" Frenchy shouted encouragement. "Don't give up now."

Billy urged his team to lean into their yokes, until miraculously they shuffled into shallower water. The oxen pitched and staggered forward. They lowed in panic.

"Quicksand!" Billy shouted. The ox beneath him wobbled and lurched. "Come on, easy! Come on!"

The team flopped and wallowed behind the lead ox. Billy kicked and yelled until he was hoarse. As if in slow motion, the lead ox shuddered, shouldered into the yoke, and hauled forward up onto the embankment. When the rest of the exhausted team and the heavy wagon arrived on solid ground, Billy slipped from the ox's back. His legs shivered so badly, he could hardly stand.

"Welcome to dry land!" Frenchy congratulated him with a

hearty thump on his wet, bedraggled head. Frenchy himself looked like a drowned rat. His shirt hung down to his pale, knobby knees.

Before Billy could offer his thanks to Frenchy, Owens shouted at them both to head back across. "Unhitch and take your team over after your other wagon," Owens ordered. "You didn't think you'd get finished so easy, did you?"

Billy glanced with exhaustion across the river at the crowd of riders, oxen, and wagons. He felt as if he'd barely avoided drowning. And now he was going to have to cross again. "Buck up, young man!" Frenchy called cheerfully. "Think of that delicious sow belly, cold coffee, and hard bread that awaits you for dinner!"

Just as Billy was about to swim his team over for the second wagon, bruised black clouds piled up on the horizon. A gust of wind blasted from the west. Thunder grumbled. Lightning spiraled.

The opposite bank seemed miles away.

"Unyoke! Unyoke!" Frank shouted.

Billy headed his team in the direction the herder was waving. He unyoked the oxen. The night herder on horseback quickly drove the team to pasture, away from the wagons filled with cargo. Skittish from the sizzling lightning, the oxen trotted with fast-paced vigor.

The wind nipped a broken board up into the air, then flipped it end over end through the sagebrush. Billy shivered as the temperature plummeted and the rain began to fall in earnest. Soggy and hopeless, he hopped from one bare foot to the other beside the wagon to try to keep warm. His boots and dry pants remained on the other side of the river, along with his valise and his other belongings. He'd hidden everything inside the second wagon. His only consolation was that he didn't have to listen to Slade and the others make fun of his predicament.

Somehow he felt certain that his father would never have been caught in such a humiliating situation.

"This is my kind of weather!" Frenchy shouted over the wind. "I scratch my head with lightning and purr myself to sleep with thunder!" He handed Billy a mangy, damp piece of buffalo robe. "Use this for warmth, boy. You look like a drowned rat." He pulled his dripping hat down tight on his head. "Going to be a real cyclone. Best find Scoundrel. He doesn't care much for monstrous big storms the way I do." Frenchy scurried away.

Billy wrapped the hide over his head and around his shoulders. His teeth chattered as he climbed into his wagon and found a place to wedge himself between crates. Pelting rain leaked through the soaked wagon cover. The wind hammered with such force that the wagon rocked back and forth as if it might tumble across the plains. Billy held tight to the wagon frame, hoping the tons of freight would keep the thing earthbound.

Covered with the buffalo robe, Billy tried to doze between blasts of lightning that blazed bright as noon. Hail pocked against the soaked wagon cover and heaped up in icy mounds all around the wagon. Billy had never seen such ferocious, changeable weather. The only thing he could think about was the valise on the other side of the river. He imagined it floating in a mud puddle or buried in hail.

*Everything's probably ruined.*

Billy slept fitfully as the storm roared. In the middle of the night a loud clash of thunder and bright lightning awoke him. Billy lay awake and worried, turning over and over in his mind all the things he did not know for certain about his father. Ma's voice echoed in his head.

*"No good sense."*

What if all the awful things she had told him were true?

*"A poor, ungodly life."*

Unease twisted inside him again.

*"Hell and flames, where he belongs."* For the first time he considered that there might be a dark side to his discovery. He knew he needed to see his father with his own eyes, just as Frenchy had said. Even so, he felt fearful.

*What would he find?*

During the night the storm finally blew itself empty. In the half-light of morning a meadowlark sang a hopeful melody. *Sleep loo lidi lidijuvi.* The rich gurgling warble awoke Billy. He peered outside the wagon and felt grateful that the storm had not been the end of the world, as he'd imagined. Cramped and weary, he climbed to the muddy ground.

At dawn Jackson and Rock had been among the first to make their way across the river. Luckily, Jackson arrived with their small trunk. He offered Billy his spare set of trousers and a pair of Rock's extra boots. In trousers too small and boots too big, Billy stood on the edge of a fathomless mud puddle. With the rest of his mess, he quickly devoured handfuls of damp bread miraculously salvaged during the storm by Frenchy's quick thinking. He'd wrapped the loaf inside his waterproof coat.

Since most of the herd had stampeded during the night, Owens assigned Billy and Frenchy to go on foot to help the herders. The herders had galloped to the east, west, and north in search of the terrified oxen. Whoever found the missing cattle was to shoot off his gun to indicate the cattle's location. Frenchy was selected because he was among the handful of drivers who knew how to handle spooked oxen.

"Owens seems to think it best to yoke an experienced one with a young, wild steer, I guess," Frenchy said, and winked at Billy. "Get up, now!"

Billy tried not to feel insulted about still being considered a greenhorn. He shifted his coil of rope to his other shoulder and shuffled along in Rock's outsize boots. Scoundrel bounded ahead, sniffing the glistening bunchgrass. The dog scared up a flock of grouse, then, as if to celebrate his achievement, rolled in a fresh pile of ox manure.

"Think we'll ever find those dang-blasted bulls?" Billy asked in a miserable voice. He wondered how far he'd have to walk before Rock's boots gave him blisters.

"Surely we will. That is, of course, unless they've run off to the ends of the earth." Frenchy shielded his eyes with his hand and stared into the distance. The herders on horseback were barely visible on the next rise. He turned to Billy. "Has all gladness left you? You seem awfully full of melancholy this morning."

Billy sighed. "I bet I lost my valise on the other side of the river. Even if I find it, the rain probably ruined everything."

"Clothes can dry from the damp," Frenchy replied in a helpful voice. "A little rain never hurt laundry."

"Wet laundry isn't what I'm worried about, Frenchy. There's a photograph in there that's the only one I have."

"Sounds like somebody special in the picture."

Billy nodded. "My father."

"I see," said Frenchy. He thoughtfully scratched his grizzled beard. "He might be richer than Midas, eh?"

"Who's that?"

"A king with a special gift. Everything he touched turned to gold."

Billy bit his lip. "Not so rich as that maybe."

"When did you last see him?"

Billy blushed. "Not since I was a baby."

"That long, eh? Well, I should think you might prepare a speech for your reunion. What will you say when you find him?"

Billy paused. He'd never thought of this before. He'd never considered how he'd introduce himself or what his first words might be when they met in person.

Frenchy whistled to his dog. "Surely your father will wonder where you've been, what you've been doing all these years. You'll give him a fright if you just turn up unannounced and blurt out your name like a bullwhacker shouting for a runaway steer."

"I suppose you're right. Do you think maybe . . . maybe you can help me practice?"

Frenchy blinked as if startled. "Here, now," he said fondly. "I'll play your father to help you rehearse for your first meeting together." Frenchy, wearing two patched shirts and a ragged pair of pants held up with a rope belt, adjusted the rope coils about his shoulders as if they were a fine swallowtail coat. He removed his battered, stained hat, curled the brim on both sides, and placed it carefully on his head. Then he stood straight and tall. "Just imagine I'm wearing a stovepipe hat and white kid gloves. And hanging from my waistcoat is a gold watch as big as a saucer—the very kind a rich miner always wears."

Frenchy's image didn't fit the way Billy had imagined his father: a loner just passing through, part outlaw, part sharpshooter, part free spirit heading west to the next frontier. "Are you sure about those gloves?"

"Absolutely," Frenchy said.

Scoundrel, as if sensing some fascinating performance, sat watching from the shade.

"Thank you, loyal secretary," Frenchy announced, turning to the dog, "for showing my prodigal son into my elegant office." Scoundrel cocked his head, then barked. "Roo-roo-roooo."

Frenchy removed from his pocket a large, soggy handkerchief still drenched from last night's storm. "This is an emotional moment." He sniffed and dabbed one corner of his eye. Then he wrung out the handkerchief so that several drops fell. "My long-lost son!" Frenchy said in a dignified, sorrowful voice. "See how well we resemble each other?"

"Sir?"

"My nose, my eye color. All yours. We have been apart these many years. Still, I recognize you as my own. My dear William, gone from me since you were a newborn child."

Billy tried hard to stifle a chuckle. "Yes, Father."

Frenchy knit his brows together in a serious scowl. "As your father, I am concerned about your wild ways and low companions. My spies have seen you with some rascals. A pigeon-hearted one who minces his steps, picks pockets, and entrances young ladies with his sweet tongue."

Billy stopped grinning. "Jackson?"

"And that other fellow, the raging one who drinks and fights? The one who has such a violent past."

"Rock, sir?"

Frenchy nodded. "And yet," he added in a thoughtful, dreamy voice, "there is one of your companions I have heard of with great admiration. That honest man, full of good advice and counsel."

"Who's that, sir?"

"He is of a pleasant disposition, generous, a stout-bodied fellow full of wisdom. He carries himself with the nobility of a knight. He must be forty years or more. What is his name?"

"Frenchy?"

"Son, he is a virtuous fellow. I have excellent judgment, though I have been negligent toward you. From this stout-bodied man's looks I can see he is kind. Keep his company. Avoid the others."

*Negligent.* Billy took a deep breath, surprised by how annoyed he suddenly felt. How dare Frenchy criticize his real father? Billy had intended this only as a game. Nothing more. He clenched and unclenched his fists and felt his ears begin to burn.

"Now let us switch parts," Billy said. Although he was smiling, his voice had an edge. "I will play my father, and you will play me."

"All right, then, sir," Frenchy replied. He placed the coils of rope on Billy's shoulders. Like a bashful, obedient son, Frenchy removed his hat and stared at his feet.

"Now, William," Billy announced in a stern voice. "Tell me where you have been."

"I have traveled a great distance to see you. All the way from Saint Joe."

Billy cleared his throat. "I have heard complaints there about you. Something about stolen money. Disrespect toward your stepfather. The way you secretly tormented your half brothers. And how you broke your adoptive mother's heart when you vanished."

"Lies! All lies, sir!" Frenchy protested.

"Now, son, you must tell the truth. For I know all, see all. There is a new companion who has befriended you. A very fat man with a mangy dog. Why do you keep company with somebody who is such a braggart and liar? What good is he to you? He drinks too much, eats too much. He is a man full of tricks and boasts, a dishonest fellow. A roaring drunk and a most picturesque and ambitious liar."

For a moment a cloud seemed to pass across Frenchy's expression. He seemed uneasy. "Who do you mean, Father?"

"He is old and gray haired. He comes from a long line of thieves, highwaymen, forgers, and pirates. A marathon talker. A buffoon. He will lead you astray."

Frenchy cleared his throat. "I know him."

"Of course you do."

"It is true that he is rather ancient," Frenchy said, as if anxious to defend himself. "It is true he is fond of whiskey and a good, rich meal—the sweeter and greasier the better. Who isn't? His background is not blue blood. But is that his fault? And if he is a cyclone of conversation, what harm is there in a long-winded story, an elaborate joke? He tells the truth mainly. Some things he stretches. He swindles some folks. But only those who need swindling. Sir, I beg you. Get rid of Jackson. Send Rock packing. But sir, do not turn out Frenchy. Kind Frenchy, generous Frenchy, entertaining Frenchy, brave and old and fat Frenchy. Keep him as your friend. Run him out of the territory, sir, and you exile all that's good and human in the world."

Billy crossed his arms in front of himself and leaned his chin on one finger—the same chilling, imperial expression of his stepfather. "I do," he said in a cold voice. "I will."

Before Frenchy could plead more on his own behalf, the herder's shot rang out in the distance. Billy rubbed his eyes for a moment. He was no longer his father. Frenchy was no longer him. "Come, booooooosss! Come, booooooosss!" echoed the familiar cry to the cattle.

"We'd better hurry and help the others," Frenchy said. He whistled to Scoundrel, who seemed to sense that something was still amiss. He whined and refused to budge. "Come along, mangy cur!" Frenchy said in an unusually harsh tone, and stormed off.

"It's all right, Scoundrel," Billy called to the dog, motioning with one hand.

Reluctantly the dog followed at their heels. It took some effort for Billy to catch up with Frenchy, who trotted along in a wounded gait. Billy could not help but feel a kind of remorse, but he turned his head away from Frenchy and said nothing. He did not know what to do to take back the harsh words he now wished he had never spoken. The two hurried across the plains, each pulling away from the other, like two yoked oxen hauling out.

# Chapter Nine

———•◆•———

LATER THAT MORNING BILLY TOOK HIS TEAM BACK ACROSS the river and found the valise—damp but safe—tucked where he'd left it inside the second wagon. Relieved, he removed the photograph and discovered that it, too, was unharmed. Secretly he vowed never again to be separated from his belongings.

"What's taking you so long? Shake a leg!" Owens shouted at Billy. Billy struggled to hitch his team to the wagon and recrossed the river. The rest of the teams followed.

During the next one hundred miles the trail headed northwest along what was once the Pony Express route between the South Platte and the North Platte Rivers. The road zigged and zagged, following Lodgepole Creek west before turning north. This route avoided the treacherous, steep hills around Ash Hollow, but for two days the wagon train had to travel without any fresh water nearby.

Owens pushed them hard, spurring the cattle on in spite of their panting and exhaustion. The land was bleached with sun. "Already nearly the end of July, and we're not even halfway there," he announced in a grave voice that evening. "If we don't make it to the Rockies by mid-August, we'll face snowbound mountain passes. And that, my friends, will be the end of us."

The next day, long before dawn, the oxen were yoked. The temperatures skyrocketed as the morning progressed. Billy wondered if his leaders would make it ten more miles. While he didn't care so much for the rabble cattle yoked in the middle of the team, he had developed a kind of fondness for the intelligence of his lead yoke, Bright and Bob, who seemed to pull willfully, even in the worst conditions.

The oxen staggered at a snail's pace across the flat, dry landscape. Their tongues hung out and they panted heavily. The teamsters knew the longer it took to cross this wasteland, the longer it would be before they reached Mud Springs, the first available water hole. The men cursed the oxen. They yelled and shouted until their voices gave out. Brandishing twelve-foot-long bullwhips, they snapped them over the faltering oxen's heads until their arms hurt. Nothing seemed to speed the oxen forward.

"The teams can't take much more of this heat," Frenchy reminded Owens when they stopped to rest at noon. "Oxen don't sweat like horses." He surveyed the long expanse of low, waterless land ahead. Even though they drove before dawn and late into the night, the heat clung to them. There seemed no relief. "You can't work an ox to death. He'll eventually stop and say to hell with you. So which is the smarter animal?"

"I know. I know," Owens said irritably.

Billy, overhearing this exchange, decided that humans were the least intelligent of all.

Under a blazing sun, with not a bit of shade in sight, the teamsters, too, seemed to stagger from sunstroke. On the long, dusty marches, when the air seemed so dry and the sun so piercing, Billy feared his brains might be boiled away by the heat.

When Billy felt most miserable, he tried to conjure in his mind what he had loved best about Saint Joe. He recalled the soft, humid summer nights when the fireflies swarmed around the bushes and the wind chanted along the quiet streets. In the darkness there had been a kind of comfort. He remembered how he had sat in the soft, cool grass and stared up at the stars and smelled the cooking coming from the kitchen and heard the sound of laughter from the houses next door. He heard piano music—the tinkling of Alice McDermott practicing for her next recital—and the *clop-clop* of a horse and buggy down the cobblestones. He thought about how the air had felt so muggy, a kind of moist humidity that made all the smells from the blooming lilacs and the phlox that grew around his house more exquisite and bountiful. The whole image gave him a sense of languid happiness.

Then Billy rubbed his sore eyes with his hands. He wasn't in Saint Joe. He was on the Plains. The brightness made him squint. When the team paused for a moment, he dipped a cup into his wagon's keg and took a small amount of water. He sipped this slowly, then sprinkled the last few drops on his kerchief. He tied the kerchief around his neck before taking his place once again beside his team.

When Owens gave the signal to start up again, however, nothing happened. No oxen moved. At the front of the line Billy heard the distinctive, bellowing voice of Rock. It was Rock's team that was holding up the rest. His pair of leaders was lying down in the yoke, refusing to get up and keep pulling.

Red faced and furious, Rock swung the whip in the air and snapped it. The biting end smacked the oxen's backs and haunches again and again. Tongues hanging out, the scrawny pair seemed barely able to lift their heads. "Get up!" Rock screamed, his shirt black with sweat. "Get up!" He pranced about and hollered like a man possessed. The welts on the oxen's backs, already lacerated, opened with dark streaks of blood. And yet they still did not move. The other cattle shook their big, horned heads.

Billy and the other men stood around, silent, barely able to watch. Each of them knew that they depended on their nigh and off leaders, the most trained and critical part of the oxen team. To beat this most precious pair of oxen was not only wasteful, it was foolish. None of the other ten oxen would be able to take over very quickly. Oxen were accustomed to routine.

"Now, what's this about?" Frank shouted at Rock. He rode up on a horse dangerously lathered in a sweat. "Get your team moving, man! You're holding up the line."

Surrounded by witnesses, Rock began to kick the oxen and snap the whip even more ferociously. A kind of uncontrollable rage had taken over. Rock's face turned redder and contorted. He shouted and swung the whip. His words made no sense. His actions seemed exaggerated and futile.

Billy recalled alley fights with other boys back in Saint Joe.

He remembered how his own anger had burned away thought and filled him with exhilaration and power. *Was this how I looked?* He cringed and squeezed his eyes shut. No matter how hard he tried to block the sight and noise, he could still hear the oxen's mournful, dying bellows.

*Smack!* An especially loud crack filled the air.

Rock howled in pain and dropped his whip. Billy's eyes flew open. "What the—," Rock screamed, grabbing his bloody right hand.

"You touch that team again and I'll give you a whipping you'll never forget." Frenchy coiled his bullwhip. From the look in his eyes it was clear he meant every word he said.

"Why, you fat old fool. You mountain of mad flesh," Rock murmured in a threatening voice. He leaned over and reached with his left hand for the knife everyone knew he always kept sheathed inside his boot. Frenchy snaked and snapped the whip again. The tip exploded with a *smack*. Rock howled and pitched the blade in the dirt. "You trying to maim me for life?" Rock shouted. He tucked his injured hands under both armpits and hunched forward. "What you boys doing, just standing there? Ain't you going to help me?"

Billy, Jackson, and the others did not move. Until that moment no one had realized the deadly accuracy of Frenchy's skill with a bullwhip. Frenchy coiled the whip again. "You remember what I warned you about beating oxen?" Frenchy said in a low voice. "Next time I won't be so polite about what patch of skin I remove from your hide." Frenchy stalked away.

"You better watch your back, old man. You're roast meat for worms. And your dog, too!" Rock said, and spat. He looked around, taking in the stares of the other teamsters. "What you fools looking at?"

The crowd of teamsters began to scatter.

"Show's over!" Owens shouted. "We got a job to do. Move around this wagon now. Get up!"

Slowly Billy and the other men got back to work. In silence they drove their wagons around Rock's fallen team. Nobody stopped to help him. Later that afternoon Billy learned that Rock's leaders had died. The pair had to be unyoked and replaced by one of his wheelers and the only healthy green steer left. Uncertain and ill-matched, Rock's new leaders had wobbled in an uncertain path.

When the wagon train finally reached Mud Springs at about ten o'clock that evening, the oxen, as if sensing the presence of water, seemed slightly revived. In spite of its name, Mud Springs appeared by lantern light to be a little run of clear water in a black, miry hollow. Cress crowded the current. Thick grass grew nearby. The moon rose. Stars glittered. Billy had never felt so tired before in his life.

While the cook fires were started, Billy took the lantern and went to the springs to fill a bucket with water. He knew enough to let the mud in the water settle a little before dipping the bucket. After several moments he held the lantern aloft and peered into the spring's black depths.

He froze.

Shimmering on the surface of the water was a startling, familiar face. The eyebrows looked so heavy, the forehead so light. Something wavered around the lonely mouth, as if his father might speak. His lips formed the shapes of sounds, but Billy could not make out what he was saying.

With one trembling finger Billy reached out to touch the sad, sunken cheek. As soon as he did, the surface rippled and broke apart into a hundred jagged reflections. The glimpsed face crumpled and vanished.

"No!" Billy whispered. He took a deep breath and rocked back on his haunches, realizing what he had seen. *That's me.* He and his father were more alike than he'd realized. For several moments he turned this surprising and terrifying idea over and over in his mind.

"Water! Hey, I need water to make coffee," Jackson shouted.

Billy plunged the bucket into the spring and hauled it to the mess.

"Took you long enough," Jackson grumbled. "What's wrong with you? You seem as if you've seen a ghost."

"I'm fine," Billy said, his voice quavering. He didn't feel the least bit hungry. His eyes must have been playing tricks. *Maybe it's the heat.*

The mess chewed the tough fried pork and drank strong boiled coffee without saying very much. Frenchy ate by himself at the edge of the firelight with only Scoundrel for company. The dog whined until Frenchy tossed him bits of meat. Billy, feeling sorry for the hungry dog, walked over and fed him his last scrap of bread. It was a kind of peace offering.

"Thanks." Frenchy managed a hopeful grin.

"You're welcome," Billy replied.

Rock, still glowering, sat with his plate on his knees. He ate with a bandaged hand. No one dared speak to him.

The next day the cattle rested. Just as Owens had predicted, the hardy oxen quickly revived. When they started moving north again, the scenery began to change. What had once been flat, sandy waste took on a strange, new appearance. A welcome relief, Billy decided. He was glad to have something to take his mind off the haunting reflection at Mud Springs and the feud between Rock and Frenchy.

In the clear, bright morning Billy spied what appeared to be a kind of massive fortress floating on the horizon to the northwest. Nearby he could make out another monolith—not as large, but equally as imposing.

After the teams waded across Little Pumpkin Creek, Billy asked Owens, "What are those rocks called, sir?"

"Court House, that's the big one," Owens replied. "Beside it is what's called Jail House."

The massive, forbidding pale rock face more than three hundred feet high reminded Billy of the biggest building in Saint Joe—complete with fancy dome, cupola, and windows. The bright sunlight and dry air created a kind of illusion so that no matter how long they traveled each day, they never seemed to get any closer to the great pile of stone.

Jackson seemed to take special delight in making sketches of the dramatic scenery. "Just like real life," one of the teamsters said with admiration as a crowd gathered to watch Jackson work during their nooning. Always the entrepreneur, Jackson managed to trade his sketches for whatever he could bargain from the other teamsters—a pair of socks, a bottle of whiskey, a bit of tobacco.

Less than fourteen miles west of Court House Rock they came upon another startling curiosity. Chimney Rock, a slender reddish column of rock on a broad mound, hovered near the bluffs of the North Platte. The three-hundred-foot-tall rock reminded Billy of the tall spire of a church back home.

"Looks like an old, dried stump, if you ask me," Frenchy said, peering into the distance. "Or the smoke pipe of a steamer."

"Reversed funnel from a still," Slade declared. "That's it exactly."

"I'd say it's a haystack with a pole stuck in the top," Tosh insisted.

"See how it's a-crumbling?" Frenchy said. "Musta been struck by lightning."

The mysterious rock formations and surrounding bluffs and buttes meant one thing. In only a few days they'd arrive at Fort Laramie.

"You make it to Fort Laramie, you can spit in the elephant's eye!" Tosh declared.

"Don't know about you boys, but I'm looking forward to some mail from home," said Jackson. He told anyone who'd listen how he was sure to receive at least several dozen letters from his sweetheart, Caddie. Secretly Billy wondered if there might be a letter there for him from his father.

The fort marked the end of the High Plains and the beginning of the long haul up into the Rocky Mountains. Fort Laramie was also commonly known as the end of the line for the tired, the sick, and the downhearted. It was here, some of the Pike County teamsters said, they'd threaten to desert. If they didn't get the wages they wanted, they'd quit. "It's as good a place as any to turn around and head for home," Slade declared.

For Billy the approach to Fort Laramie gave him a chance to

study his first real mountains. In the distance, glimmering like a cloud, he could just make out snow-covered Laramie Peak. Billy wondered how they would ever scale such heights. It seemed impossible.

Several days later the wagon train made its way over steep bluffs. At a ranch hidden in a gulch they purchased fresh replacement steers. Nearly half the oxen in each of the teams were replaced with wild, green oxen that had to be trained from scratch. Billy added only one new ox to his team.

That afternoon, while the teams nooned along a small creek, Frenchy went to work helping Billy train his new, wild-eyed brown-and-white longhorn. Billy knew that the worst thing that could happen during initial capture was to have a green steer break loose or realize its superior strength.

"If he just once learns to break the halter, no rope will ever hold him. Remember, oxen are not dumb," said Frenchy, who spoke softly as he looped the sturdy rope halter around the wary ox's head and neck. "Accept that there are some things that you can control and some you cannot."

As soon as Frenchy handed Billy the halter rope, the ox lowered its head and pawed the ground with a front hoof. The rope went taut in Billy's tight grip. "Control?" Billy asked doubtfully. "What do you mean?"

"When you train an ox, you have to remember you can only control yourself."

The ox swung its big head around, nearly stabbing Billy with its enormous horns. "Dang bull!" Billy shouted. He lifted his arm to strike the steer, but Frenchy stopped him.

"No use in terrorizing him. He's confused enough. Let him

be till he grows accustomed to you," Frenchy said. "This ox's past cannot be changed. The future is around the bend you can't see. You can only control the present. Your actions right now are what matter."

"My actions? I thought we were training the ox."

Frenchy smiled. "We are." He took the rope from Billy's hands. "Now, one of the first things you have to remember is that oxen are often far more observant of us than we are of them." He demonstrated by walking quickly and aggressively toward the steer. The animal shook its head and backed up in retreat. "You see, he's reading my mood. He sees in all directions—forward, behind, to the sides. He can catch your cues. If he thinks you're going to cause something unpleasant to happen for no reason, he becomes confused or frightened."

After much effort the rangy steer was finally yoked to a trained, seasoned ox. Frenchy hitched the pair to a stoneboat heaped with rocks. "Come up!" Frenchy barked, and tapped each ox lightly on the shoulder with a long, flexible goad stick. The loaded wooden sled weighed nearly six hundred pounds, but the trained ox dropped its neck. Pebbles flew from its hooves as it began to march.

Its green partner had other ideas. It began to shake its head and roll its eyes. The steer pulled away, as if determined to escape. The trained partner—evenly matched in weight—kept moving. Between the effort of pulling the load and being restrained by another ox, the green steer gave up the fight and wearily began to follow the other steer's lead.

"Now you try," Frenchy said. He handed Billy the goad stick.

"I never used one of these before," Billy admitted, holding the slender branch, nearly four feet long.

"Tap him on the rump and give him the cue to move forward."

Billy walloped the back of the ox and shouted, "Get up!"

"No need to holler! And you only need a slight touch to get the animal's attention," Frenchy scolded. "Many a teamster talks too loud to his oxen. And why is that? They hear as quick as a man when called for their food, which proves their hearing is good."

Billy tried again and again to teach the ox team to halt and then to move forward. Sometimes on the wrong command the green steer stopped dead in its tracks. When Billy shouted, "Whoa," the green steer kept walking while fighting its partner. Patience and consistency—Frenchy's watchwords—seemed hard to put into practice. "Won't do anything I say," Billy complained.

"Many an ox has fooled its teamster by making the teamster think he isn't listening," Frenchy said.

Billy took a deep breath. "Suppose it's the same for people, too."

"I suppose. Bring them to a stop. That's enough for now."

Billy tapped the trained steer on the nose as gently as he could. "Whoa!" he commanded. Miraculously both oxen stopped together. Relieved, Billy wiped his sweaty forehead with his sleeve. He shot a glance at Frenchy and saw that he, too, looked pleased. "I've been thinking about what you said about a fellow's actions," Billy said slowly. "About the only thing I can control—what I do right now. I'd like to clear the air about something, Frenchy."

"About what?"

"It's hard for me to say aloud sometimes," he said, and paused. "What I wanted to say was that I'm sorry."

Frenchy attached the halter back onto the green steer. "Don't exactly recall any incident." He expertly slipped the yoke from the animals.

Billy gripped the rope. Apologizing was harder than he'd imagined. "When I called you a buffoon—and worse—the day after we crossed the Platte. I'm sorry for that. And I think you should know something else."

"What's that?"

"How much I admired what you did when you stopped Rock from beating his team. That took a lot of grit."

"Wasn't much," Frenchy said, and spat.

Billy smiled. He couldn't remember when he'd ever known Frenchy to pass up a chance to brag.

# Chapter Ten

———•◦•———

"LOOKING GOOD! LOOKING GOOD!" OWENS CALLED TO BILLY that afternoon when he had his new wheeler yoked and hitched with the rest of his team. Owens rode past in a blur of dust, waving his hat to move the line forward. Although the encounter lasted only a few seconds, Billy felt delighted and proud. For the first time in his life he felt that he was accomplishing something.

He turned and glimpsed the dozen powerful, swaying oxen hauling so many thousands of pounds of goods, all under his care. If only his hooligan pals in Saint Joe could see him now! He was somebody important. A full-fledged bullwhacker.

In spite of the hardships of the journey Billy began to discover a kind of comforting predictability to the routine. Like a disciplined runner who practiced the same course every day, he knew exactly what to expect. Before dawn the oxen were yoked, the wagons hitched. This was followed by the morning march.

Next came the unyoking and nooning—a few hours of rest or greasing axles, repairing wagons. When the sun began to lose something of its midday force, the drivers would yoke the oxen again and continue the march until sunset. Each evening the oxen were set to pasture, cook fires were set, and the last meal of the day would be cooked and eaten. Sometimes somebody would sing or play the harmonica or tell a story. And in the morning the same pattern began again.

Although the pace was slow, the progress was steady. Each step, Billy knew, brought him that much closer to Virginia City. With every mile covered he was that much closer to meeting his father.

That afternoon, when the line of wagons finally reached the Laramie River, a cloud of hungry mosquitoes attacked the men and oxen. Even the biting insects did not dampen the drivers' enthusiasm. Two miles past the embankment lay the fort itself.

"Here we go, chaps!" Frank called, and plunged his horse into the shallow current.

Billy's skin had been so beaten by hot, dry sunlight that he relished the coolness of the river. The teams pulled up the embankment, past treeless hills burnished brown. Beyond shimmered the bleached roofs and walls of Fort Laramie.

"There she is!" Jackson declared.

The only grass available had been heavily grazed by another wagon train. The oxen were unyoked and the herders were assigned.

Billy, Jackson, Frenchy, and a few others hurried to give the fort a closer look. The rectangular fort sat upon a hill enclosed by a ten-foot wall, propped up in some places with pieces of timber.

While it wasn't much to look at, the fort contained a dozen frame houses, a barracks made of dried brick, a post office, a bakery, a blacksmith shop, and a sawmill. A flag flew from a flagpole. A wheeled howitzer sat in one corner of the parade grounds. The place was crowded with wagons, horses, emigrants, and dogs. More than two hundred ragged soldiers lived in cramped barracks. Every afternoon they marched in drills to the sound of a drum. Billy found this especially thrilling.

Jackson hurried toward the post office, a dimly lit shack with a crude wooden table and a heap of mail piled in a bushel basket. The clerk, who dozed in a tipped-back chair, did not seem to notice the flies that covered his hat. Billy stepped inside and scanned the walls, which were crowded with a variety of messages. Some warned emigrants of Indian attack. Others were handwritten notes from travelers looking for lost friends and family members. Several signs, curled yellow and water-stained around the edges, looked as if they had been posted for months. One poster's bright red lettering caught Billy's eye:

**$6,000 REWARD**

**FOR INFORMATION REGARDING STAGE ROBBERY**

**JULY 13, 1865, PORTNEUF CANYON**

**$150,000 STOLEN IN GOLD DUST, BULLION**

**SIX MEN KILLED**

**CONTACT H. PLUMMER. NO QUESTIONS.**

"Whew!" Billy said. "Some reward!"

"How about this one?" Frenchy said, staring at a sign on the opposite wall. He shifted his weight from one foot to the other and twisted his hat. "'Ranch for sale. Twelve hundred acres, good grass and water.'"

"That isn't half so interesting as this reward," Billy insisted. "Six thousand dollars! What's the matter with you, Frenchy? You look so greenish all of a sudden. Was it something you ate?"

"I'm fine. Maybe it's the close air in here," Frenchy said, and quickly stepped outside.

"Hope he's all right," Billy said to Jackson.

Jackson did not seem interested in Frenchy. He wasn't impressed by the red-lettered poster, either. "I'm sure they've caught the thieves by now," he said in an offhand manner. "Sir, we need to look through the mail."

The clerk pushed back his hat and tilted his chair forward. He spat a brown stream of tobacco juice onto the floor, just barely missing Jackson. "Ain't caught nobody. That's why it's still posted."

"Yes, yes, of course," Jackson said. "Can we see the mail?"

The clerk shifted a large wad of tobacco to the other side of his mouth. "Ain't even found what they did with the loot. Think it's buried someplace in the canyon."

"Yes, yes. Fascinating, I'm sure," Jackson said. "We're in a hurry." He drummed his fingers on the table as he waited for the clerk to thumb through the bushel basket of letters. "Why don't you let me search?" Jackson pawed through letters marked with only a person's name. Some owed postage. "This one looks like it's been here since Adam." He held up a yellowed letter badly mauled.

"See any for me?" Billy asked. He felt strangely hot and cold at the same time—he was so hopeful that his father had received his letter and written back.

Jackson pulled something from the heap, waved it in the air, and yodeled loudly.

Billy could barely speak. "For me?"

"Caddie, my darling, the love of my life! This letter, Slyboots, is my salvation." He hurried through the door to read in private outside the post office.

Determinedly Billy went through the letters again. Maybe if Jackson could get lucky, so could he.

"How long you going to be here, young fella?" the clerk demanded. "I'm going to dinner soon."

Billy ignored the clerk and looked through the letters for a third time. *Nothing.*

The clerk spat. "Looks like you came up empty."

"Yes, sir," Billy mumbled. He felt as if he were sliding on slick ice as he walked across the post office floor. In a daze he stepped out the door. *Nothing.* When he saw Jackson with the opened letter in his hand, his face blushed with envy and anger.

"Hey, Slyboots," muttered Jackson, who leaned against a hitching post. His face looked ashy colored even under the dirt.

"Don't say nothing to me," Billy warned. "Not one word."

"Slyboots, how long ago was June the twelfth?"

"How should I know?" Billy kicked a rock as hard as he could.

"Never trust a woman, Slyboots. She will always deceive you." He shook the letter as if it were on fire. "She married my best friend on June the twelfth."

"Who?"

"Caddie." Jackson crumpled the letter in his fist. "I'm never going back to Rutland. Never."

"Jackson!" Rock called. He hurried closer and fanned himself with his hat. "Any word?"

"Just my death sentence, that's all," Jackson said in a dull voice. "My life is over. She's married."

"I don't mean word about *her*," Rock said impatiently. "I mean is there any news about the job?"

"Nothing," Jackson said, and wiped his eyes with his handkerchief. "I need a drink."

"What are you talking about?" Billy demanded. "You fellows find somewhere else to work? Does Owens know? He's going to be awfully mad."

Jackson kept shaking his head. "I can't believe it. I told her to wait for me. I told her I was coming back."

"What are we going to do, Jackson?" Rock said in a low, desperate voice. "He was supposed to write to us here, wasn't he? Now what are we going to do?"

"Why do I have to do all the thinking?" Jackson demanded angrily. He stuffed the letter into his pocket. "He can go straight to hell. So can she." He stumbled away.

"What's wrong with him?" Billy asked Rock.

Rock shrugged. "Women."

*Well*, Billy vowed to himself, *I'll never act so foolish.*

When the wagon train left Fort Laramie the next day, the men and oxen followed a rough and stony road that would lead them to the North Platte River ford. Along the way stood the biggest trees Billy had seen since they left Saint Joe. A grove of cottonwoods, some already burnished yellow, shimmered in the wind. At noon they found a hollow with thick grass. Just as they began to eat their first meal of the day, a warning call rang out from one of the herders.

"Indians!"

The men grabbed their guns. Somebody pointed toward a bluff. Billy stared in the distance, expecting to see a fierce war party bristling with shields, lances, old flintlocks, and brightly decorated horses. Instead, approaching their camp at a leisurely trot were an Indian and his squaw. The man was wearing a fancy red shirt, a gaudy yellow vest, and an old felt hat. The woman carried an umbrella over her head. Coils of brass wire and bands of silver circled their arms and fingers. Around the man's neck hung four pairs of spectacles. Each horse pulled a travois, a carrier made of two poles. Piled on top of the travois were their belongings and a dismantled tepee. A pair of snarling dogs brought up the rear.

"Nothing to be afraid of," Frenchy said in a confident voice. "Why, I met a few Ottos in Nebraska, and I can tell you what. You just don't let them fool you, that's all. I've had plenty experience with warriors. Just have to use common sense, that's all."

The Indian raised his hand as if in greeting. "Show some hospitality," Owens warned the others. "I think they're just looking for some handouts."

The visitors settled in around the fire that had been started by Owens and his mess. The woman sat apart from the others and ate hungrily from a plate of beans and salt pork balanced on her lap.

Frenchy swaggered over to the campfire where Billy, Rock, and Jackson were boiling coffee. "You can be sure I'd have some jolly times among the Indian squaws!" Frenchy boasted. "I know their sign language."

"Is that so?" Rock asked, stifling a chuckle.

"You seem to be an expert about the romantic inclinations of the red-skinned female population," Jackson said. "Why don't you go over there and introduce yourself to Mistress Umbrella? I have heard that they are especially fond of men of substance, such as yourself." He nudged Rock with his elbow.

Frenchy hitched up his sagging pants and adjusted his hat. "Well, I suppose I will." He made his way across the camp to the next mess.

"Greetings, strangers," Frenchy announced. He made some elaborate hand gestures. The man and woman ignored him and kept eating. "Welcome!"

Frenchy at least had the good sense to bring along his own tin cup of liquor. He took a quick swallow, wiped his mouth with the back of his hand, and heavily lowered himself to the ground. He sat cross-legged a few feet from the woman. Jackson and Rock sidled closer for a better look at Frenchy's performance. Billy felt embarrassed for Frenchy. Didn't he know he looked like a fool?

Although he had failed to get the young woman's attention, Frenchy persisted. Using signs and words, he proclaimed crudely his romantic intentions. "Enough moon talk!" he declared in a voice far louder than necessary for someone sitting so close to him. "Will you be mine?"

The woman finished eating her salt pork and wiped her hands on the grass. Not once did she look at him. The Indian man took hold of Frenchy's arm and drew him toward her.

Frenchy, clearly surprised, yelped and tried to leap away. "Wait a minute!"

The other teamsters hooted. Jackson laughed so hard tears streamed down his face.

Again the Indian man grabbed Frenchy. "I don't mean to offend you, sir," Frenchy protested. This time he couldn't seem to wriggle free, and his face turned pale with terror. "No, no. I don't want to. Not here. I changed my mind."

Slade and the others howled with laughter.

"You played out, Frenchy?"

"Must be too much alkali water!"

"Don't start what you can't stop!"

The Indians rose to their feet. With a look of disdain, they remounted their horses and headed south toward the river.

"Now, Frenchy, that was a very bad idea," Rock murmured.

Jackson nodded. "I believe you'll soon regret your actions."

"What do you mean?" Frenchy said nervously.

"You have given that warrior offense by your refusal of his woman," Jackson replied. "He will surely avenge the insult."

"Oh, what do you know?" Frenchy insisted. "You're only trying to frighten me."

Jackson and Rock exchanged meaningful looks. "Don't say I didn't try and warn you," Jackson said.

That night Billy spied Frenchy buckling on his pistol. In the darkness Scoundrel began to howl. When Frank went to inspect, he announced to Billy and the rest of the crew that he had spied the Indian who had visited them earlier that day. "I say," he said, half grinning, "that same bloke was prowling around the outside of the corral. When I came closer, he hid under one of the wagons."

"Which one?" Frenchy demanded.

"I'm not certain," Frank said.

This seemed to be all that Frenchy needed to hear.

"Where's Frenchy?" Rock asked Billy later when it was his turn to stand guard. "He's supposed to take over after you're finished."

Billy shrugged. "Haven't seen him."

When Frenchy did not appear hours later, when the moon rose and wolves began to howl, Billy circled the camp looking for him. *What if he's been ambushed?* Billy inquired among the others if they'd noticed Frenchy's absence, but nobody seemed to care.

"He'll turn up in time for grub," Rock said.

In the morning Frenchy staggered back into camp. He looked pale. His clothing was disheveled and his white hair stood out in tufts.

"Where have you been?" Frank demanded in a stern voice. For once he seemed to be enjoying his role as authority figure.

"Herding," Frenchy mumbled.

"Herding? That can't be, old bloke," Frank replied. "I was herding, and I didn't see you."

Several of the men began to laugh. "I was there," Frenchy insisted, his face bright red. When he filled his cup with coffee, his hand shook so badly he spilled most of it on the ground.

"Rock, weren't you supposed to haul more water?" demanded Jackson. He poked the feeble fire with a stick.

"I was busy," Rock said with a smirk.

Jackson stood up, hands on his hips. "Where were you?"

"Herding," Rock replied.

Everyone laughed except Frenchy.

As they came closer to the North Platte ford, the road became increasingly littered with parts of broken-down wagons and other debris. It seemed to Billy that every overloaded outfit ahead of them must have decided to jettison extra weight before they reached the river. Wheels, axles, and wagon trees lay helter-skelter among spilled crates of horseshoes, a feather quilt, one heavy wooden bookshelf, and a fancy painted globe. In haphazard heaps lay a wig, a pair of ladies' shoes, and a glass lamp. Travelers had thrown away bags of flour, burlap sacks of salt pork, a barrel of rice, and a putrefied side of bacon. Among the cast-off furniture, tools, and food were bleached bones of oxen and rotted mule carcasses that filled the air with a sweet, sickening stench.

"Look at this!" Billy shouted. He'd found glistening in the sunlight a round piece of glass in a brass fitting inserted inside an elegant wooden box. He ran to Jackson to show him. "What is it?"

Jackson didn't take much interest at first. "How should I know?"

Billy held up the box and looked through an opening in the back. "Makes everything upside down."

"Let me see that thing." Jackson took the box from Billy and peered inside. "Remarkable!" It was the first time Billy had seen him look genuinely happy since before Fort Laramie.

"You can have it," Billy said generously, still not understanding what the object was.

"A camera obscura," Jackson said. "A tremendous find! It's used to record images. A little like a camera lens."

Billy smiled. He wanted to appear as if he'd known all along.

After descending some steep hills at dusk, the wagon train approached a Mormon emigrant camp. From a distance the numerous campfires and cooking fires made the place look like a miniature city. As the train grew closer, Billy could see encircled almost every kind of conveyance, from hand-drawn two-wheeled carts and carriages to heavy covered wagons. Most of the rigs appeared patched and ancient. Three hundred emigrants had gathered inside the circle of wagons. Someone sang a plaintive song. A violin and harmonica played. Entranced, Billy paused and listened.

"Look at that," Jackson said, waving in the direction of the encampment. Dancing in a circle were four young women, laughing and twirling with their arms locked. He stopped and stared. The wagon train abruptly came to a halt.

"Keep moving!" Owens shouted. "Get up!"

A woman's high, shrill giggle filled the air. "Come on, Jackson," Billy called. Instinctively Billy rubbed his neck and recalled what had happened to him on board the *Denver*. He could still feel the knife blade biting into his skin. "Jackson, move!"

Jackson finally shuffled along beside his team. He plodded with his shoulders sagging, his back bent.

The next four days were a long, hard drive over red and dusty hills. The country, Billy thought, had become as desolate as anything he'd seen. There was little vegetation to speak of, nothing but weeds, red clay, and jagged rocks. The road headed north and west along the southern edge of the North Platte. They had passed the entrance for the Bozeman Trail, the most direct route to Virginia City. The Bozeman angled northwest along the Bighorn range, cutting through the most dangerous Sioux country, controlled by Chief Red Cloud.

"There's good grass and water on the Bozeman, but no out-fit has gone through in the past year without being ambushed," Owens said to the assembled group of teamsters. He intended instead to take the longer, safer route. They'd continue west past the Salt Lake City cutoff and then veer straight north along the Idaho Gold Road to Virginia City. "We'll be adding two hun-dred miles or more to the journey, but we're more likely to arrive with our scalps."

"That's an extra two weeks, maybe more," Rock grumbled.

"Nothing would please me more than the prospect of dan-ger and excitement," announced Frenchy.

"You old windbag!" Jackson replied. "You don't care because you hardly got any hair to scalp!"

Everyone laughed and hooted. Frenchy took off his hat and bowed to display the shining top of his head.

While Billy felt disappointed realizing how much farther they still had to go, he was secretly glad not to face any more danger than they had to. It seemed to him that they'd be lucky to make the hard pull up the steep hills and mountains that lay ahead without a smashup.

That evening at supper, after a particularly difficult climb, the cook in each mess passed the word. "Sugar's run out. Boss says we've used up our rations." This message had a kind of electric effect on the teamsters, who immediately began to com-plain. Sugar was one of their only luxuries in their coffee. They had more than three hundred miles to go and nowhere to buy more.

"No problem," Rock said in a conniving voice. He disappeared from the campfire for a few moments and returned from his wagon with a large sack of sugar, the bag still sewn shut.

"Better not, Rock," Billy murmured.

"You're a fine one to talk," Rock replied.

Billy squirmed, recalling the way he'd taken his stepfather's money. What Rock was doing seemed different somehow. Maybe because Billy respected Owens.

"Stealing from the cargo's going to land you in big trouble," Tosh warned. "You gonna get yourself horsewhipped."

"I ain't afraid," Rock said smugly. He took his knife from his boot and slit the bag. Then he wiped his spoon on the back of his pants and dug into the sugar. He dumped three heaping spoonfuls into his coffee. "Who wants some?"

At first no one moved. They'd been warned repeatedly about stealing from the cargo.

"What's the matter with you cowards?" Rock insisted, grinning.

"Guess stealing sugar's as easy for you as highway robbery," Frenchy said in a low voice. "Or murder, maybe."

The fire crackled. Coffee suddenly boiled over from the pot on the fire. Nobody bothered to move. Nobody breathed. Nervously Billy scanned Rock's face, which had turned a dark, dangerous color. Why, he wondered, couldn't Frenchy keep his big mouth shut?

"You poisonous, hunchbacked toad!" Rock shouted. He leaped through the air and knocked Frenchy to the ground. Dust flew.

"Get offa me!" Frenchy howled. He lay pinned on his back.

Scoundrel barked. The dog nipped ferociously at Rock's pants, causing Rock to let go of his hold on Frenchy. Frenchy wriggled free, while Scoundrel tugged and tugged until the seat of Rock's pants tore clean away.

"Ow!" Rock screamed. "I'm gonna kill that dog once and for all!" He reached for the knife that he kept strapped inside his boot. Before he could make a stab at the dog, a shot rang out.

Owens replaced the revolver in his holster. "What's going on here?"

"Nothing," Rock said. He gave the dog a swift kick and pulled down his shirttail to cover the ripped seat of his pants.

"Just a misunderstanding," Frenchy said. "I believe I soundly beat and set this young whippersnapper in his proper place."

"You miserable fibber," Rock muttered.

"Who stole the sugar?" Owens demanded. He pointed to the slit bag that sat in the firelight, slumped forward like a dead man.

Nobody spoke.

"You expect us to work like dogs for this food?" Rock demanded. "You have plenty more sugar in the cargo."

Owens scowled. "I know who's already taken more than his share. And you can be sure the amount will be deducted from your pay."

The group of drivers gathered around the fire began to talk and complain all at once.

"Take our pay? What pay?"

"It's slavery. That's what this is."

"We should take what we need and to hell with this outfit."

Without warning another shot echoed through the air. Billy flung himself into the dirt with his arms over his head.

"You rascally looters, listen to me!" Owens shouted. "Anyone who steals from my stores will pay back every penny."

"Every penny!" Rock said, and spat in disgust.

"That's right, Rock," Owens said. "I know this ain't the first time you've been stealing sugar. And the way I calculate it, the amount you've taken will eat up almost all your wages and then some."

"Is that so?" Rock said in a menacing voice. The other men standing between Rock and Owens stepped back nervously. "Who is going to make me?"

"I'm wagon boss," Owens said in an even voice, and replaced his revolver in its holster. "Not you, Rock."

Rock grinned, but he never once took his eyes off of Owens's gun. "Hear his threats, boys? He can starve you and me any which way he pleases. Well, I'll tell you something, Mr. Wagon Boss. I ain't paying for no sugar. I ain't paying for nothing. I'm walking off this miserable job."

"Where do you think you're going to go?" Owens demanded. "How long you think you'll survive on the road before you run into some war party?"

"I'll take my chances," Rock said.

Billy watched Rock stalk off to the wagon for his belongings—all unpaid for.

"You put those traps down," Owens said in a steely tone. "They belong to me." He and the others watched Rock return to the firelight with his arms filled with clothing, shoes, and a blanket.

Rock quickly slipped his hand inside the bundle. His pistol flashed into view. He pointed it at Owens. "I don't think so,

Owens. I think they're mine." Owens stepped back and let him pass. "You coming, Jackson?" Rock demanded. His face had a wintry, boulder-jawed quality to it that Billy had never seen before.

"I changed my mind," Jackson replied.

"Why?" Rock demanded. "We've come this far—"

"I'm out. I'm not going."

"Two-faced liar."

"My dear Rock, are you threatening me?" In the dim firelight Jackson's smiling face looked as false as a mask. For the first time Billy wondered if Jackson might actually be afraid of Rock.

Rock mumbled something to Jackson that Billy could hear only in snatches. "Ninth gate . . . ain't going to like this . . ." Rock turned briefly to Billy. "How about you, Slyboots? There's easier ways to make a fortune than eating dust with this outfit. You want to join me?"

Billy avoided Owens's flinty gaze. He knew Frenchy was watching him too. Virginia City was still miles away.

"No," Billy said. "I'm staying."

"Suit yourself, Slyboots," Rock replied. He tipped his hat, then vanished into the darkness.

"Can't say I'm going to miss that beetle-headed, flap-eared knave," Frenchy declared. "Good riddance."

"I hope the blackguard don't give the rest of you any ideas," warned Owens, who ordered extra armed teamsters on herding detail. "I don't trust that rogue. He may be lurking about."

That night coyotes howled. A light rain began to fall and the wind blew. And even though Billy placed his Colt under his pillow, he still couldn't sleep.

# Chapter Eleven

———•◆•———

IN THE MORNING, BEFORE DAWN, THE CALL WENT UP TO yoke the oxen. Owens was in a hurry to get the wagons across the famous Platte Bridge. The seven-year-old bridge was said to span the turbulent Platte River with one thousand feet of cedar logs lashed together on cribs filled with stone. "We won't be getting our feet wet this crossing, boys!" Tosh said.

"Let's just hope she holds," Jackson replied. Everyone had heard about the Indian attack a year ago, when three thousand Sioux, Cheyenne, and Arapaho had ambushed a small government wagon train. When two dozen soldiers from the 111th Kansas Cavalry came to the rescue, only three escaped alive by drifting downriver camouflaged in the debris of the burned wagons and cargo.

"We need to move across the Platte as quickly as possible," Owens announced to the assembled teamsters. "Rumor is that the Indians are beginning to play the deuce around about. I've heard that they've attacked and taken Fort Reno on the Bozeman Trail."

Billy gulped. They were going into hostile territory now, that much was certain. He glanced about the silent group of teamsters. Whatever excitement they'd shown about crossing their first bridge seemed to have evaporated.

Rock's team had been yoked and his wagons were hitched. Frank was assigned to drive the extra rig. After they paid the toll, they moved without incident across the bridge. On the other side the road was lined with sagebrush and prickly pear, sand lily and blazing red Indian paintbrush. They raised dust past the crude wooden grave marker of A. H. Unthank, who had died July 2, 1850. His grave marker said simply: KILLED BY INDIANS.

"A bit of bad luck, eh?" Frank called to Billy.

Billy did not find the joke the least bit funny. He kept wondering what had happened to Rock. Was he following them?

"Make way! Make way!" someone bellowed.

Four horses heading east with four soldiers in faded, patched Union uniforms galloped past. The riders whipped their horses hard and vanished.

"Where they off to in such a hurry?" Billy asked Frenchy.

"They might be messengers. Who knows?"

Not long after, three teams of mules pulling wagons charged past, heading the way Billy and the others had just come. The mule teams trotted as quickly as beasts pursued by the devil himself.

"Where you going?" Jackson shouted.

"Deer Creek telegraph station!" the driver hollered back. "Burned to the ground."

"More Indian trouble, I guess," Frenchy told Billy. He scanned the surrounding hills. "Maybe the telegraph men are going to repair the line."

Billy did not reply. They had just passed Deer Creek the day before. Danger might be closer than he'd realized.

The next afternoon they passed a small, tumbledown sod house. A man perched on a bench. He leaned, half tilted to one side, against the sod house wall. Behind him was a crude window. A red scrap hung in the opening, the remains of a battered curtain. There was no sign of a chicken, a cow, or any other living creature to be seen, yet somewhere nearby a dog barked. Trudging along at the end of the line, Billy thought the man was asleep, until he called to Billy. "Hey, pilgrim!"

"Yes, sir?"

The man tipped upright, stood, and ambled closer. Billy, bored and dusty, welcomed any company—even someone who kept scratching as if he'd just slept in a nest of chinches. "How long you been gone from the States?"

"Couple months maybe," Billy said. "How about you?"

"Couple years maybe. What you carrying?"

"Dry goods mostly, for Virginia City."

The hawk-nosed stranger craned his long neck around to inspect Billy's dusty wagons, half covered with ragged canvas tarps. "Reckon you're a smart young fella. Maybe we can do some business."

"What kind of business?"

"The drop-by business."

"What's that?"

The stranger shielded his eyes from the sun and glanced up and down the rest of the line. "Simple. I'll give you money if you drop a coupla those bags off the back of your wagon when you get past Sweetwater Station. A little grove of cottonwoods just past the footbridge over the crick. Can't miss it. Just keep moving along. I pick up what you drop by. Then I'll bring you ten dollars by the time you get to the first cutoff. The whole thing will look like an accident, see? Your boss will never be the wiser."

Ten dollars was a lot of money. And yet there was something unsettling about the stranger, who appeared as if he had not had a bath since he left the States. "I have to pay my boss for what's missing out of my wages," Billy said. "I could stand to lose a great deal. What if I refuse?"

The stranger pointed to a nearby butte. "My partner's a good shot even from this distance."

Billy squirmed and tried to peer through the cloud of dust. He couldn't see anything. If he was caught stealing, he'd owe Owens money. Billy imagined himself pathetic and dead broke by the time he arrived in Virginia City. What would his father think?

"Don't make sense to give up living and breathing for some other man's dry goods, do it?"

Billy couldn't even see the wagon ahead of him anymore, the dust had become so thick. "I'm not interested," he said. "Sorry, sir."

"Hey, Billy!" Frenchy called. "You seen Scoundrel?" Billy was never so delighted to hear Frenchy's voice as he was at that moment. Frenchy took one look at the stranger and demanded, "Who are you? A new recruit?"

"No, sir." The stranger squinted at Frenchy, who was cloaked in such a thick layer of reddish dirt his grizzled mustache and beard had turned pink. "Just trying to make a little business deal. Ain't you—"

"No, I ain't," Frenchy replied quickly. "And this young gentleman is letter A, number one—above par a very great way. So I recommend you make yourself scarce double quick, because I am the best shot on the prairies or in the woods, and I can shave the eyebristles off a wolf as far as a shooting iron will carry a ball. You understand me? Now, get!"

In an instant the stranger vanished. Billy felt relieved and embarrassed. "Thank you, Frenchy," he said.

"Remarkable what a reputation for deadly strife will do to frighten off the addle brained," Frenchy replied. "There's my Scoundrel! I hear him now. Remain wary of swindlers, my boy. This country is rife with them."

For the next several days the teams followed the north side of the North Platte, until they reached a branch of the Sweetwater River, where the road continued west. The Sweetwater wasn't as grand as its name, but the silvery trickle of fresh water seemed a blessing in a place where grass grew only in sparse tufts on sandy, alkaline soil.

The oxen, half starved and overworked, began to drop to their knees, unable to take another step. Billy's team was reduced to five yoke—only ten exhausted steers barely able to pull the load of two wagons. Without enough oxen power, the wagon train faced the danger of being stranded in treacherous

Indian country. No replacement animals could be bought at any price between here and the next trading post, Fort Bridger, nearly one hundred fifty miles away.

Carcasses of oxen and mules lay strewn along the road. Some were fresh. Some were picked clean. Overhead circled buzzards. Their shadows drifted past again and again. That evening Owens told the men to anoint the sore hooves of the cattle with grease and gunpowder. Frenchy showed the drivers how to cut the hides of dead oxen into strips and wrap and tie these around the hooves of the teams that were left. Billy took pieces of rags and cast-off clothing he found along the way and fastened these under the yokes of his oxen to help ease some of the ugly sores on their necks. There seemed nothing anyone could do, however, to lessen the suffering of the starving oxen. Their sad bellowing all night long kept Billy awake and filled him with dread. *How much farther?*

By the time they reached Horse Creek, not only the teams but the men were exhausted and hungry. They had run through all the fresh oxen meat they'd collected. Not once had they seen any of the famous herds of buffalo Billy had read about in the *Morning Herald* back in Saint Joe. The overworked men were too tired and slow to hunt successfully the herds of nimble, big-eyed pronghorn that veered past and then raced at breakneck speed over the next rise. Small game such as rabbits and grouse was often the best any of the drivers could hope for. "I'd settle for fried prairie dog," Jackson complained. "Anything but more salt pork."

"Amen," echoed Frenchy.

•   •   •

During the next week of travel the wagon train followed a route west that sometimes seemed as confused as a frayed rope. In places the path was twisted tight in one obvious direction. Other times the trail flayed apart, as if uncertain which way to go. The road was rutted with parallel tracks, two wheels, four wheels, eight wheels wide. The trail wove in and out of fording places, crossing and recrossing the Sweetwater as if it couldn't make up its mind which side to stay upon.

Interconnecting with this braided, unbraided skein of paths were cutoffs and shortcuts. These sometimes appeared on official maps, where they were called Lander Cutoff, Sublette Cutoff, Hudspeth Cutoff, and Bear Ridge Cutoff. Some were simply advertised along the way with crude wooden signs promising GOOD ROAD or CLEAR WATER.

At each branch in the road there was much discussion and debate among teamsters and emigrants about the best direction to travel. Which route avoided hostile tribes, detoured around dry, waterless stretches, or skirted impassable hills and mountains? Drivers like Owens, who had been this way before, claimed to remember the pile of rocks, the cleft in the mountain, the place the fastest, safest trail detoured and picked up again beyond the bend. Billy and the others had no choice but to follow Boss and hope for the best.

After passing the great, crouching outcropping called Independence Rock, the road turned away from the Sweetwater. The struggling river slipped north into the steep, cavernous Devil's Gate, a narrow cleft in a granite mountain. Once again the wagons were forced to follow a route through dry, bare sand hills where no water could be found for miles. The grass of late August was dry and brittle.

Billy's mouth was sore and his lips were cracked. It seemed to take enormous effort to put one foot in front of the other and walk alongside the stumbling team. The oxen leaned against their yokes and slowly pulled the wagons up the incline that veered sharply to the left in an S-shaped curve. The sand and rocks had been so eroded by previous years of rainfall that the road was almost too narrow for the width of the wagons. As the oxen trudged slowly upward, the ravine to Billy's left seemed to drop deeper and deeper. The hooves of the oxen knocked loose gravel, which clattered down the incline and bounced and crashed onto jagged boulders below.

Billy knew there would be barely enough room for the wagons to pass because of the tightness of the first turn. His desperate hope was to force the leaders up onto the slight, sandy bank to the right and hold them there until the wheelers at the end of the line had a chance to complete the first turn.

"Gee! Gee, Bright and Bob! Whoa!" Billy shouted to the leaders to pull right onto the bank and then stop. Bright and Bob bellowed. Chains clanked.

Billy scrambled nimbly between the line of oxen and the ravine's edge to reach the wheelers at the end of the team. He tried not to look down. He had to make sure that the wheelers made the sharp left turn and then pulled as far as they could to the right to clear the wagons. He had made it only halfway down the line when Bright and Bob bolted. The leaders rushed downhill on the next curve, yanking the rest of the oxen around the precipitous left turn. Pointers and wheelers stumbled on the edge of the ravine, barely able to keep their balance.

"Whoa! Whoa!" Billy yelled. He plunged to his knees, gripping a crumbling rock ledge as nearly five tons of oxen pounded past, sand flying. The wagons teetered, out of control. A grinding metallic noise sheared the air. Billy watched in helpless horror as the left rims of four sets of wagon wheels slipped and slid to the ravine'e edge, teetered, and dropped. Four axles thudded, touching ground. The two overloaded wagons tipped and hung frozen, four right wheels on land, four left wheels in space. Chains thrummed and strained as the oxen, pulling what had suddenly become an immovable object, had no choice but to stop.

Billy barely breathed. *"Your actions . . ."* He imagined in slow motion how the heavy wagons would tilt, tumble, and—*". . . right now . . ."*—drag him and the oxen over the edge—*". . . are what matter . . ."*—plunging in a crushing, tumbling avalanche of animal flesh and splintered wood crates and cascading white sugar and shattered whiskey bottles and . . .

*No!* Billy blinked. He heard Frenchy's words again. *"Your actions right now are what matter."* In that instant he scrambled to his feet. He gripped one of the wheelers by his horn and shouted to him and his yoke mate, "Gee! Gee!" He punched his whipstock into the wheeler's ribs and with all his might forced them to pull the teetering wagons back up onto the road. The oxen bellowed. Billy rushed toward the leaders, screaming, "Easy! Easy!"

The team inched forward, and the wagons barely made it around the curve. "Easy! Easy!" Now the road headed down an incline. As the team pulled, the wagons rolled faster and faster, shoving against the oxen. "Whoa! Whoa!" Billy shouted, his voice nearly giving out. For once the weary oxen obeyed.

He grabbed from each wagon a set of chains, which he wrapped around the back wheels so that they remained locked in place. "Easy! Easy!" Billy snapped the whip in the air as the exhausted team shuffled down the steep hill. The creaking wagons sledded through gravel and sand until the team safely reached the bottom, a flat stretch of road where Jackson and three other drivers and their teams were already waiting.

"A true oxman!" Frenchy said, smiling. "You passed muster, yes sir."

Jackson waved his hat. "Nothing to it, right, Slyboots?"

Billy's shirt was sodden with sweat. His face was streaked with dirt, and for the first time he noticed how his knees and hands were trembling. Even so, he felt happy. If only his father could have seen him. *A true oxman.*

By the next afternoon they were headed over the highest hills they had yet encountered. The road snaked and switchbacked. The air was fragrant with the spicy smell of low-clinging juniper and stunted pine. To Billy it seemed as if they'd entered a region of clouds. Mist concealed the valleys below them. A raw westerly wind bent and shook the trees. Billy pulled up his coat collar.

"Look there!" Slade shouted. To the west the clouds suddenly parted. For a moment the drivers stared at the white gloaming on the horizon. Billy quickly realized it wasn't a cloud formation; it was the white, unmistakable wall of hundreds of snow-covered peaks.

"There's the Rockies!" hooted Tosh. "Get ready now, boys. Ain't nothing taller where we're headed."

Shivering, Billy gripped his elbows. His only surviving clothes were a thin pair of pants, worn-out boots, a threadbare shirt, and a light coat and hat. He had no socks, no gloves. He tried to imagine how he'd survive in those cold, stormy mountains. The teams had barely struggled this far. How would they ever manage to cross the steep, snow-smothered passes that lay ahead?

"Enough of your confabulating!" Owens shouted. "Move out!"

Billy stuffed his hands in his pockets. "Get up," he called to his team. "Come on, now."

After several days of hard drives the wagons reached South Pass. The broad valley was nearly twenty miles wide. Steep mountains fenced it on each side. Snow covered the far summits. At midday they stopped to let the oxen graze.

"This is supposed to be the Continental Divide? Ain't very impressive, if you ask me," complained Slade. Billy had to agree. There wasn't anything especially dramatic about the valley covered with sagebrush. He'd expected a narrow passage walled by rocks hundreds of feet high. The divide didn't seem any steeper than the slope outside his old schoolhouse.

"A toast with a rare brew!" Frenchy said. He held in the air a cup of water.

"What's that?" Billy demanded.

"The waters of the Atlantic mixed with the waters of the Pacific," Frenchy replied. He took a sip. "Delicious! I might bottle such a fine elixir and make a fortune."

Billy and the others watched the approach in the distance of a familiar group of travelers. The Mormon wagon train had managed to catch up with them again. Because the Mormons had lost a number of their cattle, many of the women and children were walking to lighten their wagons' loads.

"Gracious ladies," Jackson announced, and removed his hat before a group of giggling, barefoot girls. "Would you like a ride?"

Three sisters from London seemed delighted to sit on the crates of goods in Jackson's slow-moving wagon. The other teamsters, noticing Jackson's success, invited several young ladies to ride along. By the time they reached the Green River and made a long, difficult crossing, Jackson appeared to have fallen in love again.

On the other side of the river, after eating a delicious meal of roasted potatoes that were a gift from the Mormons, Jackson took a seat in the grass beside Billy. "I have quite settled in my mind," he said in a low voice, "that I shall leave this outfit and go to Salt Lake."

"Salt Lake?" Billy whispered, surprised. "With the Mormons?"

Jackson nodded, smiling. "I have you to thank. I'm giving up my former unlawful life. I intend to become a photographic artist."

Billy studied Jackson's radiant face. Former unlawful life? Was this another one of his tricks?

"After I told a certain charming young lady about the camera obscura you found for me and described my talents, she assured me that I can obtain good employment in her uncle's studio," Jackson explained. "It seems that the Mormons like nothing better than to have their likenesses recorded."

"What happened to getting rich in the mines and returning to Vermont?"

"I told you I'm never going back. My future is in the West." Jackson plucked a long piece of grass and chewed the end. "Bullwhacking's too arduous. Hard-rock mining will be even worse. I am not suited for such harsh employment." He examined his callused palms and fingers. "These are an artist's hands."

"You never stick with anything very long, do you?"

"Never say never," Jackson said, and winked. "The man who adapts survives, Slyboots. Say, why don't you join me? Salt Lake City will be a golden opportunity. The chance to return to civilization and find rewarding, lucrative indoor employment while keeping your scalp intact."

"Can't go with you," Billy said slowly.

"Don't tell me you like this miserable job," Jackson said, and took the grass from his mouth. "I saw how you handled that team back there on the steep road. You're fast on your feet and quick thinking. You're resourceful and tireless. Just the kind of fellow I admire. And there's no use pretending that traveling alone to Salt Lake City is a safe proposition. We can help each other."

Billy shook his head. "I still intend to find my father in Virginia City."

"Slyboots, you're a stubborn stampeder. What in the name of heaven do you think you're going to find?"

Billy bit his lip. "Maybe I just want to see him, see what he looks like. Tell him I'm all right."

"Let sleeping dogs lie, that's what I say. What point is there in finding out some awful truth? You'll have to reinvent yourself, you know. Everything you thought about who you were won't fit anymore. I prefer my own illusions about myself."

Billy's heart pounded in his throat. "What do you mean?"

"I only hope your father doesn't disappoint you. We can't pick our parents, can we? I always wanted a different father. An educated gentleman with property—not a drunken, poverty-stricken bricklayer. To live, dear Billy, is to forgive. I wish you the best of luck." Jackson stood up and brushed off the seat of his pants. "Let me know if you change your mind and decide to join me. No hard feelings, I hope?"

"Nope," said Billy, still stunned. Some awful truth—was that what he would discover?

"Don't take what I tell you too seriously, Slyboots. You know I'm an inordinate talker and a terrific liar."

The next morning Jackson announced his plan to leave the wagon train, and as Billy had expected, Owens became rip-tearing mad. He let loose with a stream of profanities and oaths, swearing hell and damnation. "You'll come with me or you'll be arrested when you get to Bridger. I'll make sure they haul you to jail. May you rot in hell!"

Jackson gathered up the few things he owned. To travel light, he abandoned his trunk and tucked his possessions inside a burlap feed sack. He set off after the Mormons, who seemed to be on their way toward the nearest ranch at Blacks Fork.

With a sad, sinking feeling Billy watched Jackson head up the first rise. He knew deep down he'd never see him again. "Hey!" Billy shouted after him. "Hey, Jackson!"

Jackson paused and turned.

"You got the camera?"

Jackson held up his thumb. "You bet, Slyboots. Take care of yourself, now."

Billy waved. First Rock had left, now Jackson. *We were supposed to be partners.* Overhead wheeled a lone killdeer that whistled a sharp, mournful cry. Billy felt the skin prickle on the back of his neck. When he looked again to the rise in the distance, Jackson was gone.

# Chapter Twelve

THEY LEFT THE MAIN TRAIL SIX MILES WEST OF DRY Sandy and headed west. The wagon train crossed the Little Sandy and the Big Sandy and struck off toward the Green River again. Owens spoke of nothing but Lander Cutoff and how it would save them time. "I hear it's a fifty-mile shortcut," he claimed.

They climbed higher and higher until they entered a place filled with trees. After crossing the icy Green River, water seemed in abundance everywhere Billy looked. There were streams, lakes, creeks. At night the thin air was cold enough for Billy and the others to see their breath. Billy felt revived after having escaped from the dust and dry heat of the plains. It seemed to him anything might be possible. Soon, he was certain, they'd reach Virginia City. At last he would find his father.

The wagon train followed the edge of the Bear River into a high, green valley. Already the aspens were beginning to turn golden. The sky during the day was clear and blue, and yet Owens seemed frantic to keep moving as fast as possible. Any moment, he said, they could be hit by snow.

At the northern bend of the Bear River they came upon Soda Springs, where cold, fizzing water boiled directly up from the earth. Beer Springs was what Frenchy dubbed the spot. The water tasted acidic. Tall, fantastic rock formations, some crusty red, some darker, had grown around the gushing springs. Like so much of what Billy had seen since he'd left Saint Joe, Soda Springs seemed a kind of strange wonder.

That evening the wind blew cold and wintry. Billy, Frenchy, and the others huddled around a roaring wood fire. "How far to Virginia City?" Billy asked Frenchy.

"Maybe two hundred miles," Frenchy said, and took a swig from a jug. Scoundrel curled up around his feet. "The wagons still have to reach the Snake River, then head north."

Slade whistled. "Our first real town, boys! Pass me that red-eye, will you?"

Frenchy handed him the jug. "Hope you're not expecting anything too impressive. Virginia City's so new the clapboard and log buildings aren't even weathered. Some are so jerry-built they're already collapsing. It's the only place I ever been where there's a law what says: 'Houses not built in the middle of the street ain't to be disturbed.'"

"How come you ain't your usual braggy self, Frenchy?" Slade said, and nudged Tosh with his elbow. "I'd think you'd be full of grand stories about glittery Alder Gulch."

"Just want you fellows to know what you're in for," Frenchy replied. "Virginia City is crawling with thousands of people.

Just don't want you to get lost and befuddled, that's all."

Billy gulped. "How do you find somebody in particular in such a busy place?"

Frenchy scratched his chin. "Walk straight to the spot where Wallace Street and Jackson Street meet. That's Content Corner. You'll see Content's store there. A two-story building right in the center of town. As I recall, if you traipse up Wallace Street, you'll come to the Gem Saloon, the only decent stone building in town. Across from the Gem is the big Idaho Hotel and Billiard Parlor. Avoid these places if you can. You remembering all this?"

Billy could feel his cheeks burn. "I still don't understand," he admitted, "where . . . where I go to find my father."

Frenchy stared into the fire as if lost in thought.

"Frenchy?" Billy asked softly.

"Content's," Frenchy said. "He'll know where to find your pa among the b'hoys. Content knows everybody. Well, fellows, tomorrow is another busy day. Best get some rest. Good night."

Relieved, Billy gave Scoundrel a pat on the head. *Content's.* That seemed easy enough to remember. He watched Frenchy and the dog amble into the darkness.

During the cold, gray hours before dawn the teams were yoked and hitched to head west from Soda Springs. The air smelled of snow. The sky looked dark and threatening. They had reached a confusing land of contorted rivers. Some flowed north, others drained south. Perhaps because of the weather or the confusing watershed Owens seemed especially anxious to get the wagon train under way. Just as they were about to depart, Frank galloped into view. "We can't leave yet, Boss," Frank said.

"Why not?" Owens demanded impatiently.

"Frenchy's missing."

"Maybe he's drunk again. Somebody check his wagon," Owens said. "Can't I count on anybody in this outfit?"

"Already looked in the wagon, sir," Frank said. "His dog's missing too. No sign of them."

Owens took off his hat and smacked it hard with frustration. "Anybody see him this morning?"

"Not me, Boss," said Slade.

"Sir, I haven't seen him since last night," said Billy, who was beginning to feel worried. Where could he have gone?

"What about you, Tosh?" Owens asked.

"Boss, why you looking at me like that? I don't know nothing," Tosh insisted.

"He'll be back, I'm sure," Frank said. "Isn't a better driver in the outfit. He's usually first to have his team yoked and ready to go."

All morning the men puttered around the camp greasing axles and making repairs to the wagons. Meanwhile Frank and Owens, on horseback, surveyed the Bear River embankments for any signs of Frenchy or his dog. Billy searched Soda Springs and walked up and down nearby creeks calling for Frenchy. He found nothing. When Owens and Frank returned to camp, their discouraged expressions revealed that they'd had no luck.

"How could somebody just vanish like that?" Owens asked, shaking his head. "He was the best hand I ever had. Well, we can't wait here any longer. We've got to get moving." Owens set off to tell the others.

"Never trusted that fellow," Slade said when he heard the news.

"His begging dog was a pest," agreed Tosh. "That creature stole food out of my wagon. I saw it with my own eyes."

"I never believed that story how he found Scoundrel in an otter trap," said Slade. "Nothing but a liar."

"Frenchy," Tosh said with authority, "was possessed of more egotism and vanity than I ever saw enclosed in so fat a compass."

"What if he's injured?" Billy protested. "What if he's been shot by Indians? What if he's sick?"

"Don't worry about that sack of wind," Tosh said. "Nobody could kill him if they tried."

Billy squirmed. He didn't like the sound of Tosh's joke. What if Rock had been following them, just waiting for his chance to get rid of Frenchy? Everyone knew how much he despised Frenchy.

Finally Frenchy's team was yoked and his wagons were hitched. Frank was assigned to drive the extra team as the lead rig. As they set off on the road, Billy gazed desperately into the trees. Frenchy had disappeared before. He had always returned. Any moment Billy expected to see Frenchy coming around the bend. Scoundrel would bound and leap and bark, and Frenchy would laugh at them, as if the way he'd vanished was just a joke.

"Let's go! Head out!" Frank shouted.

Reluctantly Billy followed the others back to the road for a

hard drive over steep hills. After so much hard labor they'd covered barely ten miles. That night it was Billy's turn to serve
herding duty. As usual he intended to take along his Colt. But
when he searched the valise, the gun was gone.

"Anybody seen my gun?" he asked Slade and the others.

"Bet Frenchy took it," Tosh said.

Billy did not want to believe that Frenchy would stoop so
low. How could he do such a thing? Angry and unarmed, Billy
made his way to the pasture.

The cattle chewed and moved among the sage. Overhead
the stars gleamed with a kind of painful, piercing brilliance. A
moonless night. Billy wondered where Frenchy might be right
now, and he silently cursed him for tricking him into thinking
he might be his friend. That he might help him find his father.

Billy roamed among the dark shapes that were cattle, careful not to move to quickly or to spook any creature unexpect-
edly. The oxen tore away what little they could find among dry
tufts of grass, chewing loudly. The oxen lifted their heads. Even
in the darkness he could sense the way they listened intently.
Something howled and yipped; it sounded like crazy laughter,
like the mad yapping of a wounded dog.

Coyotes.

Three or four slipped among the sagebrush. In daytime coyotes were known to dart across the dry plains, their gray brown
coats blending into the brush, bushy white-tipped tails flared.
At night they moved with a kind of fearless swagger. This was
their time to hunt. Billy automatically put his hand in his
pocket, then remembered his gun was gone. The coyotes
passed.

Wind winnowed the trees and grass. Billy sat on a flat rock, pulled his coat around himself, and dozed. When he came awake suddenly, he heard something nearby.

*Crash!*

Billy froze, wondering if it was Indians. They would run off horses or mules before they'd try to stampede oxen. But if they were hungry enough, even an ox might be worth stealing.

Billy whistled to the other herder. Nothing.

Odd.

He whistled again.

"What is it?" Frank called. The sound of his voice seemed reassuring.

"You hear something?"

For a moment there was silence. "No, I don't. Maybe it's the bloody wind knocking branches about."

Billy bravely walked around the herd twice, three times. He told himself he needed to restore the circulation in his legs. When he was satisfied that there was nothing threatening nearby, he resumed his spot on the flat rock.

He missed Scoundrel and his earsplitting warning howl.

After a tedious drive the next morning the wagon train followed a wild river that cascaded beneath a cliff. Clouds of steam rose from quiet pools. The hot springs smelled of rotten eggs. "What an awful stink!" Slade said when the wagons halted near a series of mysterious holes in the ground that emitted smoke. In several places thick mud bubbled like pea soup in a kettle.

Billy could tell something was wrong. Owens, who usually

seemed confident about where they were going, had stopped three times to consult a worn map he kept in his saddlebag. The rumor quickly spread among the men that they'd taken a wrong turn after they left the Bear River outside of Soda Springs. By now they should be able to see Mount Putnam dead ahead—not the entrance to a canyon. "Looks like devilish country if you ask me," said Tosh, surveying the smoke holes.

Without warning an eastward-bound wagon—the first they'd seen for two days—barreled into view. Owens hailed the driver. "What's ahead?"

The red-faced driver halted his mule team but seemed none too pleased by the delay. "Portneuf. Some call it Robber's Roost."

"The canyon hideout?"

"That's the place," the driver said. "Every sort of bandit and Indian ambush. We were lucky to make it through. Six stage-coaches filled with gold from Alder Creek and bound for Salt Lake have been attacked in the canyon in the past three months. If you're headed for Virginia City and you have a lick of sense, you'll turn back and take the other route that follows the Ross Fork to the Snake River." The driver snapped his whip and urged his team forward again.

Billy felt a rising sense of dread. *Frenchy.* What if he'd stumbled into trouble in dangerous Portneuf?

Cautiously Owens announced that they'd turn the teams and head back the way they had come. "We've lost two days or more, but we don't have much choice. We'll noon here along the river, then reyoke."

"Not a spit of grass," grumbled Slade, who'd been

assigned herding duty. The oxen, too, seemed anxious about the grumbling sounds coming from the smoke holes. Before Slade could hobble the leg of Owens's best horse, a spurt of steam vented from the ground. The horse reared and galloped away in terror. "Hey! Hey! Catch that horse!"

As the horse disappeared into the canyon, Owens exploded with every cussword known to the teamsters and a few they'd never heard before. "Can't I count on anyone? We can't afford to lose that horse, and we can't afford to send another horse and rider after it. What else can go wrong?"

"I'll go, Boss," Billy said, hoping to impress Owens.

"You?" Owens seemed surprised.

"He's fast afoot, Boss," admitted Slade. He glanced at Billy as if grateful.

Tosh nodded. "He can take my rifle."

Owens glanced toward the canyon. "All right, then. You're going to have to hurry. If you're not back by sunset, Billy, we leave without you."

Hastily Billy grabbed a coil of rope, Tosh's rifle, and a chunk of bread. He took off at a lope, filled with exhilaration. They were all watching him, he was certain. Especially Owens. This was his chance for greatness.

The air was thin, and he found he became more winded than he'd expected. But he kept running, slapping one foot down after the other and hefting the rifle in his right hand. The ground was solid, pockmarked stone, brittle and unrevealing. On such a hard surface there were no signs of hoofprints, only the occasional rut of a wagon wheel. How was he going to track a trackless horse?

Billy's heart thumped like wingbeats as he ran. The shadows of canyon walls fell upon his path, and he kept moving, aware now that the others could not see him—that he had vanished from their view. He was alone.

It seemed strange to be covering ground by himself. He had become so accustomed to traveling in a group. *"Oxen are herd animals."* That's what Frenchy had once told him. Was he becoming a herd animal too? He wasn't certain if that was a good thing.

The river howled and bounded along beside the narrow road. The noise of the rumbling Portneuf River echoed with a constant rushing refrain. How could he hear the nickering of a runaway horse or the sound of hooves against rock? Besides, if he shouted, could anyone hear him?

The farther he ran, the more he became aware of the canyon walls. The sky had vanished except for a slit of bright blue overhead. He had grown accustomed to open vistas—first the level, boundless plains, next the mountain valleys, the high upsweep of butte. This was different. The canyon crowded around him with a kind of damp, dark coolness. His pace slowed to a trot, and he wiped his nose with his sleeve. For one moment he glanced up and froze. The profile of a head.

Somebody was staring down at him.

Billy darted full-speed behind a rock. He hunched there, vulnerable and terrified. When would his heart stop pounding? *Nobody. It's nobody.* He gulped and peered upward. The shape had vanished.

*Just a tree moving in the wind.*

Billy grabbed the rifle and took off in a sprint. Sweat trickled down his arms, his back. He glanced ahead, desperate for the sight of a swishing tail, the rolling black gleam of eye, the roan-colored flank, the sleek darkness of a leather saddle. Somewhere just ahead, he prayed, the horse was grazing contentedly. *Can't be far.*

He hoisted the rope to his other shoulder and shifted the heavy rifle. He wanted so badly to return in triumph with the saddle horse. In his mind's eye he saw how Owens would grin, how he would pat him on the back and say over and over, "Looking good. Looking good."

Billy tried to ignore the way his calves began to throb. He tried not to think about how the holes in the soles of his boots seemed to allow every sharp rock to pierce his feet. He was accustomed to running barefoot on soft, grassy ground—not sprinting on slippery rock in worn boots. But he kept running.

The canyon changed as Billy headed deeper and deeper. The spires of limestone and shale, the walls and innumerable crevices, towered on each side. Rocks arched like enormous doorways. Others stood like pillars. The shapes reminded him of chimneys and haystacks, church pews and locomotives. Some rocks looked like buildings half torn down. To keep from feeling so fearful, he named what he saw: Old Hen with Her Chicks and Dragon Head and Giant Toadstool and Elephant Rock and Old Woman.

He spied the entrance to a smaller side canyon. On the ground meandered a dry-wash gully strewn with rubble. Billy paused. What if the horse had followed this branch of the labyrinth? He passed the side canyon's entrance and kept walking, searching the ground. At last he found what he hoped was a sign: a pile of fresh manure. Maybe ahead he'd find the horse.

Anxiously he loped along the main canyon. His eyes searched each rock, each jutting formation. He told himself he was hunting for the horse, praying that he would not have to follow one of the branches. *Hideout. Ambush.* Who knew who might be lurking? Maybe warriors. Maybe thieves. He ran faster.

His fear, he discovered, goaded him on to new speeds.

When he reached a major split in the canyon, he stopped. Tall rocks with fat tombstone shapes rose up in the middle of the cleft. Around the base the rocks were riddled with low caves, as if they'd been worn away by the flow of another long-ago river. While the road and Portneuf headed up in one direction, the other cleft in the canyon offered the washed-out path of a dry creek bed. Which way?

Above the sound of the roaring river he heard a sharp, pure song purling in the canyon air. *Yew, tiyew, tiyew, tiyew.* The bare cascade of sound stopped. Where was the bird? Was it watching him? Billy stood in a shadow, breathing hard. His damp shirt clung to his back. Who else might be watching him? The skin over his cheeks and forehead chilled, as when sweat suddenly dried. He shivered.

*Yew, tiyew, tiyew, tiyew.* The silver song lilted this time with a kind of final grace note.

*Decide.*

He had to pick one or the other canyon route. If he picked the wrong direction, he'd eventually have to backtrack and follow the other. Billy lowered the rifle and the coil of rope to the ground and gazed at the shadows. From the slant of light he considered that it might already be late afternoon. The idea of spending the night in the canyon seemed horrifying. Boss expected him by nightfall. Desperately he glanced along the nearest rocks. If he climbed the tallest spire as fast as he could, he might be able to save time and see what lay ahead. Maybe he'd even spy the horse.

He looked up. He'd climbed the church steeple back home as a prank with his friends. If he could scale the heights of the Baptist church with parts of the minister's carriage on his back, he could certainly skylark this rock. With new determination he scrambled up one broad boulder and then another. For one second he glanced over his shoulder and saw below him the dizzying red gold riprap of river rock and the high yellow of aspen. He stuck the slick toe of his boot in a crevice and pulled himself higher.

The wind began to blow and the rocks made a whistling sound. How much time had passed? He had to hurry. Billy found a foothold on the side of a large rock. He shimmied up, groping for the next ledge with one hand and moving his foot about to locate a foothold. Then another and another. Higher and higher he clambered.

At one point he paused to blink. If only he could wipe the grit from his eyes. But he couldn't. He had to hold tight. When he reached for the next ledge, the rock crumbled. Pebbles tumbled down, and for a moment his sweaty hands slipped. He threw himself forward, caught his balance, and grabbed another ledge in time to pull himself up.

Finally he reached the top of the enormous rock. Before he knew what was happening, a gust of wind tore off his hat. The hat soared crazily, then plummeted—becoming smaller and smaller, until it was a mere speck as it landed on the canyon floor far, far below.

Billy's heart galloped in his throat. How high had he climbed? Instinctively he crawled on his hands and knees away from the rock's edge. He paused, pressed his cheek to the warm, rough granite, and closed his eyes. Gradually his heart stopped racing wildly. He was safe.

When he sat up, he was aware for the first time of the power and the vastness of the canyon, and the mountains and meadows beyond. It was a world marked by broken rock, shadow, brittle sagebrush, and high summits covered with snow.

Clouds scudded along the great arc of blue sky. Their shadows galloped across the canyon, where rocks caught the changing light and created a pattern of burnished red, brown, and yellow. A pair of hawks circled lazily above a ridgetop of pines, twisted and small and wind whipped.

To the west glinted stark white peaks. He turned to the south and gazed out over the rocky shapes of spires, turrets, domes, and hollows that seemed fantastic and macabre. To the east, more mountains—and beyond these he knew lay Saint Joe and the Missouri River, too far for him to see. A place that now seemed like some distant, half-forgotten dream.

Billy took a deep breath, marveling at the spicy, sweet smell of pine and sagebrush and the clean, dry air that filled his throat and lungs. He felt a kind of exhilaration. No longer trapped inside the canyon, he could finally really see. As he gazed around in all directions, he thought he could spend the rest of his life here atop this rock, just watching the play of light, listening to the keening wind. He felt big and small at the same time. How was it that the dizzying sweep made him for one moment seem as enormous as a towering mountain and the next as puny as the smallest insect?

The sun had dipped closer to the western horizon. He didn't have much time. A raven glided past and called a deep, taunting *Brooonk*. Billy scanned the two branches of the canyon. Deep below in one branch he thought he saw a metallic flash along the pale thread that he knew was the Portneuf River.

Was the flash from sunlight on the horse's silver bridle?

Something twisted in his stomach. He had to get down before the horse bolted again. He couldn't stay here forever. This whole thing had been a terrible idea. He cursed Owens. He cursed the others who had not volunteered. They'd abandon him if he did not get back by nightfall. Then what would happen to him? He thought of Frenchy and how easily the outfit had left him behind. *They'll do the same to me.*

A cool wind picked up the dust. Anxiously Billy licked his lips. The sky to the west had begun to turn a dark, sullen color. Cool wind crooned. He scrambled to his feet and walked to the edge. This was the place, wasn't it? He had to get down before the storm. As he hesitated, far below he heard a horse whinny. Peering over the side, he saw the unmistakable shape of the horse galloping deeper into the canyon. The horse's saddle flapped wildly.

*Boss will kill me.*

Urgently Billy turned, lowered himself to his knees, and felt over the edge for the first foothold. He gripped the rock ledge with his sweating hands, and carefully used his other foot to reach down for the second, then the third. The wind buffeted. How much time? How much time before the storm hit? He grappled with the next ledge, the next rocky outcropping. For a moment he glanced toward the distant ground. He gripped the ledge and squeezed his eyes shut, sick with dizziness.

*Open your eyes.*

He glanced down and moved his toe for another hold, another ledge. The ledge crumbled. Small rocks cascaded and bounced. At the last possible moment he clutched the nearest ledge, his left foot probing for another toehold, however small. He found one and pressed against it, hoping it would not give way. *Keep going.* His chest tightened. His feet and hands refused to move. In his mind's eye he saw again how much space yawned between him and the rocky ground below.

*I can't do this.*

For several moments he clung there, not looking at the ground, not moving—simply frozen in terror.

Wind howled. The sound jolted him into action. He lowered himself another step, then another, coaxing himself down, telling himself if he had made it up the cliff, he could make it down. Just thirty feet more, twenty more. He glanced down and saw a ledge flat enough for one foot. Cautiously he reached out with his hand for balance, catching a ridge. Just as he gripped it, just as he sensed it would hold solid, he heard near his head a dry rasping, a furious shaking. The sound he had heard a hundred times.

The warning of an angry rattlesnake.

Billy flinched and pulled back his hand. And in that moment he lost his balance.

*No!*

His back arched despite his desperate tries to throw his weight forward to grab anything, any piece of rock, any blade of grass, any root. He kept falling. His arms flailed. He felt nothing as he bumped along the rough rock face. It was as if he were watching himself from a distance—how he struggled stupidly, how the ground kept growing closer and closer. There was nothing he could do to save himself, but he kept trying.

"Slyboots! Slyboots!" voices jeered. He saw Rock and Jackson and the rest of the outfit standing on the ground, waiting for him to land. They stood in rows, beefy arms crossed in front of themselves, looking disgusted. "Slyboots! Slyboots!" He saw Owens, Frenchy, and his stepfather, angry and impatient. "Slyboots! Slyboots!"

Just as he was about to shout and defend himself, darkness swallowed him.

# Chapter Thirteen

⬩◆⬩

SLEET PECKED AGAINST THE DRY GROUND. ICY WIND LASHED the owl clover and balsamroot that rustled near Billy's face. In the distance came the hollow roar of moving water. Closer, perhaps only inches from his head, something whined. The high-pitched, incessant noise made him open his eyes. He still saw nothing except darkness, and he wondered if he must be dead. *Where am I?* Billy tried to remember. He blinked hard again and again. Only blackness. He moved his hand to brush away the awful, earsplitting noise.

A soft, wet mess of evil-smelling fur pressed for one moment against his skin. Instantly Billy recoiled in terror. *Coyote? Bear?*

A cold, moist nose shoved against his face, then burrowed into his coat pocket. Billy tried with all his might not to breathe, not to move. The animal found what it was looking for—what smelled like a piece of bread—and began to chew vigorously with its sharp, clicking teeth.

Finally, thinking better of the idea of playing dead, Billy shouted, "Get! Get away!" His voice was only a croak. He twisted onto his side to sit up and flee. A violent pain shot down his arm, his leg. His whole body felt sore and bruised. Even so, he struggled to stand. When he did, his leg collapsed under him. He crumpled in a helpless heap.

The sound of the circling wild creature seemed to be getting closer again. "Get away!" He tried to sound fierce, hoping somehow this might scare it away. But the animal seemed undeterred. It panted and complained, padding back and forth, so that its paws made soft, sucking sounds, as if it was walking in water or mud. Every so often the wading creature would pause and whine.

Billy shivered with cold. His clothing was soaked. His leg throbbed. When he looked up, he noticed something like pricks of light overhead. He wondered if they might be stars. Or perhaps they were the swirling shapes he'd seen just before passing out on the steamboat. Would that be better? Just to fall unconscious?

*If it's going to eat me, I don't want to be awake.*

Stubbornly the animal kept circling. And somehow Billy remained conscious. Finally he reached into his pocket and found the last remaining soggy crumbs and hurled them at the animal. He was only buying time. Once the creature became tired of gnawing bread, Billy knew that he would be devoured next. He lay down on the moist ground and waited. Too tired, too wet, too filled with pain to run away or resist.

The creature whined again, then barked: "Roo-roo-roo-roo."

The loud, ferocious noise was unmistakable.

"Scoundrel!"

The wriggling dog threw himself on Billy. Even though its fur, tangled and wet, smelled of something like skunk and mud and dead fish, Billy was never so glad in his life to embrace Scoundrel. Tail wagging and thumping wildly, Scoundrel slobbered and twisted, leaped and danced in dog joy. "Where's Frenchy?" Billy demanded. "Where's Frenchy?"

Scoundrel only continued his joyful dog dance. Billy glanced around in the darkness, convinced that if Scoundrel was nearby, his owner must be too. He called again. "Frenchy? Frenchy!"

No answer.

Billy didn't want to think about the awful possibility. What if Frenchy wasn't alive?

Billy shivered. And then he remembered where he was. Portneuf Canyon. He had been climbing, looking for a lost horse farther down the canyon, when he fell. Billy grimaced with pain. Then something wet and cold began to cling to his face, his lips, his hair. With dread he held out his hand.

Snow.

He knew he had to find some kind of shelter. He couldn't stay out in the open all night or he'd freeze to death. Calling to the dog, Billy crawled as best he could on his hands and knees to search for one of the caves he remembered at the base of the rocks. Someplace to hide from the wind.

As he scuttled through thorns and jagged stones, he was overwhelmed by his own foolishness. His arrogance and stupidity in climbing that rock seemed boundless, incredible. He had failed completely. Owens and the others had probably left without him. He'd lost everything. His precious photograph, his valise, and all his belongings. He'd lost his job, his chance to find his father.

His feet throbbed from stone bruises. His arms ached from thorn punctures and scratches. With one hand he tried to feel where he was going. A crevice, a crack, a slight rocky overhang. Anything at all. After many attempts he finally discovered what seemed to be a kind of round-shaped burrow in the rocky wall. Exhausted, he crawled inside. Scoundrel curled up against his chest. Billy slept, grateful for one salvation: the kindness of a warm dog.

When the first light appeared, Billy woke up stiff and sore and half frozen. Several inches of snow had fallen—and Scoundrel had vanished.

"Scoundrel!" Billy called. "Where are you?" He was certain he had not dreamed the dog. A windswept trail of paw prints zigged and zagged toward the river. There was a place where it looked like the dog had been digging. Billy struggled to his feet. He leaned against the rock, unable to put any weight on his other foot. Already he could see how his ankle had swollen. How would he make his way back to the wagons?

The strange, tall rocks loomed desolate and forbidding. "Scoundrel!" he shouted. His voice drowned in the echo of the roaring river. He hopped once, twice, to look for the rifle. He did not even feel the cold as he frantically scooped away snow. *Where is it?* Each place he looked, he found nothing. Was this the right place? Or this?

Finally, after furiously scooping, he felt cold metal. The rifle.

He swiftly dug it up and, cradling it in his arm, considered firing a shot. Maybe the others were looking for him. Maybe if they heard the shot, they'd know where he was. When he attempted to fire the rifle, though, he discovered that it was jammed.

*Dang Tosh!*

He emptied the cartridge chambers and placed the bullets in his pocket. The only thing the rifle was good for, he discovered, was as a crutch. Leaning on the rifle, he hobbled away from the wagon road toward the river, following Scoundrel's paw prints. Snow-laden shrubs surrounded the river, edged in some places now with ice. Billy's feet were cold. The sky was gray and somber. The air smelled as if it might snow again. He knew he was going to need to build a fire.

Using his rifle to balance himself, he leaned over and picked up pieces of dead wood and branches and began throwing them into a pile. He bent over to tug at a log. Suddenly he lost his balance, slipped, and tumbled flat on his back.

*Blam, blam, blam.* A series of shots rang out.

*I'm saved!* Billy felt certain Owens and the others were coming for him. Before he could scramble to his feet out of the tangle beneath the bush, another volley of shots echoed through the canyon. Then another. Billy ducked and remained flattened against the snowy ground.

These were no warning shots of rescuers. This was a gun battle.

Someone shouted. He heard the clattering of horse hooves. Another shout. More shots. Two horses trailing harnesses in tandem, with a man riding bareback, hurtled past. He pressed his body low against the horse, clinging to its neck. The pair of horses slid crazily in the snow, followed by a large black horse whipped hard by a man in a long, waterproof beaver coat. He carried a rifle. His face was partially concealed by a bandanna, which he'd tied over his mouth and nose. For one moment as he galloped by, the rifleman stretched up his head and tugged away the bandanna, as if to take better aim at the fleeing bareback rider. As he did, Billy could see his distinctive boulder jaw, his furrowed brow.

*Rock!*

Stunned, Billy watched as two more men hurled past, riding at breakneck speed. These he did not recognize. He noticed only that each carried a carpetbag strapped to the back of his horse.

Billy could barely breathe. *Stage holdup.* Somewhere along the road a stagecoach had been attacked. What was clear was that the stage driver, riding bareback on part of his team, would never escape alive.

Billy struggled to stand. *What if they come back? What if they see me?* Desperately he grabbed the useless rifle, and with the barrel pointed to the ground, he placed the stock under his arm and used the gun as a crutch. Uncertain where to go and what to do, he hopped along the snowy road in the opposite direction of Rock and the others. Among the hoofprints in the snow he found reddish spots scattered here and there.

Blood.

For a moment twirling shapes danced in front of his eyes. Billy feared he was about to faint, when distant gunshots rang out.

*BLAM, BLAM, BLAM.*

Rock was a crack shot. Billy felt certain the bareback driver was dead. Billy jumped and began to hobble along faster. Every so often he frantically looked behind himself to make sure the gunmen weren't returning. If they'd taken the loot, why would they need to come back in this direction?

Billy followed the snowy horse hoofprints around the next bend and then another. In a narrow clearing near the river a stagecoach lay overturned on its side. One heavy wheel continued to spin slowly. Someone's arm rested outside the open stagecoach window. The black-gloved hand rested on the door, as if at any moment someone might pull down on the handle and step outside.

Billy hobbled closer, past tangled harnesses and a pile of envelopes and papers fluttering from a ripped canvas bag. "Hello?" he whispered. "Are you all right?"

The arm did not move. Billy tiptoed on the driver's box using his one good foot. He managed to pull himself with his arms atop the overturned coach and stared into the open window. Three bodies of men, each shot in the head or neck, sprawled inside the stagecoach. Blood was splattered everywhere.

Billy backed away, slid from the side of the coach, and landed in a heap in the snow. He bent over and vomited. When he lifted his head, he heard a high, shrill whine. Slowly, carefully, he managed to pull himself back to his feet. *Somebody's still alive.* Billy wiped his mouth with the back of his hand, picked up the rifle, and glanced around. Strewn about the wreckage he spotted a hat, a whiskey bottle, an enormous beaver-skin coat, a leather pouch turned inside out, two shattered bottles of Parker's Ginger Tonic, and scattered bits of pipe tobacco.

"Roo-rooo-roo-rooo!"

"Scoundrel?" Billy shouted. The barking was coming from the river. He hopped and slipped and skidded in that direction. In the snow trailed more footprints, strewn with blood in haphazard patterns. "Scoundrel!"

Beyond a shrub the dog whined and barked. When Billy came closer, he found a body crumpled beside the icy water. The man's hat lay beside him. With a shaking hand Billy gently lifted his shoulder. The heavy body flopped onto its back. Although his mouth and nose remained concealed behind a tied kerchief caked with snow, his brow and bald head were unmistakable. "Frenchy," Billy murmured.

Stunned, Billy kneeled beside the body and pulled away the kerchief. Frenchy's cheeks were nearly as pale as his white whiskers. His lips had turned a bluish tinge. Still gripped tightly in his fist was Billy's stolen Colt. As Billy attempted to take the cold gun from his hand, he noticed that the left shoulder of Frenchy's dark blue coat was soaked with blood.

Billy tried not to look.

The dog whined and pawed his master, nudging against his great belly with his snout. Every so often the dog would stop and stare at Billy, as if to demand he do something.

Billy did not know what to do. He felt a terrible surge of sadness. "Why, Frenchy?" he sobbed helplessly. "Why'd you have to die?"

"Aw, quit your caterwauling," Frenchy said. His blue eyes flitted open. "Where's my hat?"

Billy nearly jumped out of his skin. "You're alive?" He wiped his eyes. "Why'd you scare me like that?" he demanded angrily. "You stole my gun. Why'd you run off? What were you doing?"

"My last job," Frenchy whispered, with a faint grin. "Needed the money to buy cattle for the ranch. Never was a decent highwayman." For a few seconds his eyes shut.

"Frenchy?"

"Needn't shout. Ain't deaf."

"Was it Rock I saw on horseback?"

"Yep. Said I was a bungler. He was right."

Billy glanced over his shoulder. What would he do if Rock and the others came back looking for more loot? "We've got to get some help for you. Don't worry, everything's going to be fine."

"He wanted Jackson, but he bowed out. So he let me come. And I went, for old times' sake. Got something to drink?"

"Sorry, Frenchy. Don't have a thing."

Billy knew he couldn't lift Frenchy. He was too heavy. He'd have to rig up some kind of sled to move Frenchy away from this place where they were certain to be found. "You stay right here with him, Scoundrel."

Billy hobbled back to the stagecoach. He nearly tripped over the driver's sleek beaver-skin coat. The slick surface of the coat gave Billy an idea. He managed to unbuckle several long lengths of leather harness that had been cut away by the driver. He tied two sections to each arm of the coat, which he dragged to the river. With great pushing and shoving he managed to roll Frenchy onto the coat. He placed Frenchy's hat on his head and tied the harnesses around his own waist. Billy leaned with all his might to sled Frenchy along the riverbank.

"Get up! Get up, now!" Frenchy shouted.

"Very funny," Billy grumbled. He slipped and slid trying to get traction using his one good foot and the end of the rifle dug into the snow. Luckily he found another small cave around the next two bends. Scoundrel scouted ahead while Billy dragged Frenchy to the mouth of the shelter. He paused, out of breath. "You are too stout, Frenchy. You know that?"

Frenchy did not answer. He had closed his eyes again. This alarmed Billy. Was he freezing to death? He hurried to gather as many branches, small twigs, moss, and pine needles as he could to start a fire. Without flint or matches, he had no idea how to start a fire. Glumly he tugged Frenchy as far as he could inside the cave. He untied the harness attached to the beaver-skin coat. At least he could cover Frenchy with this. "Frenchy?" he said softly. "Can you hear me? You gotta get up and just walk a few feet inside to this cave, see?"

"I need a drink," Frenchy murmured.

"Come on, Frenchy. Get up and walk. Just a little ways." Billy pushed him until he sat up.

"How about a smoke?" Frenchy said, wobbling to his feet. "My shoulder hurts. Can I have a smoke?" With much effort he trudged inside the cave and sat down. "Cold in here. Can I have a smoke?"

"Sure, sure. And how about a big roast beef dinner, too?" Billy said with irritation as he picked up the coat. Something rattled inside the folds of the coat. Eagerly he stuffed his hand in the pocket and found the driver's box of matches wrapped inside a woolen scarf—still dry. *Lucky.*

With shaking hands he lit the little mound of branches and

started a fire. He fed it carefully with more small twigs and moss. Slowly the flames grew. He added a small branch and then another.

Soon the small cave began to feel warm. The firelight cast shadows on the back wall. Frenchy groaned, and Scoundrel glanced up from the nice, warm spot he'd found in front of the fire. Although Billy did not know the first thing about wounds or bandages, he tried to think what to do. What had Ma done the last time he'd scraped his arm when he fell out of a tree? Something with water and soap. She'd cleaned the wound, hadn't she? Billy wished he'd paid more careful attention.

He went outside and gathered a pile of snow inside Frenchy's hat. When he returned, he carefully ripped away the cloth near the shoulder of Frenchy's bloody coat. Billy had to use all his concentration not to pass out in the presence of so much blood. He hummed the tune to "What Was Your Name in the States?"

*Steady, steady.*

With care he made a ball of snow and pressed it against the wound.

"Ow!" Frenchy shouted. "You call that good nursing? I'm a mortally wounded man. I need a drink."

"Please be quiet," Billy said. He used the soggy muffler to clean what he could from the wound, then he wrapped Frenchy's shoulder with a torn piece of sleeve from his own shirt. "There. Soon you'll be good as new." He tried to sound cheerful. But he knew their prospects looked dire. How long before anyone passed along the road who might rescue them? What if he couldn't hobble into sight fast enough to call for help?

To keep his mind off their troubles and his own throbbing leg, Billy searched outside for more sticks and logs. Snow began to fall softly again as he dragged these inside. "More snow," he said in a cheerful voice. "At least it'll cover our tracks."

Frenchy only grunted. "Look in my coat pocket."

"I'm sure you haven't got a jug in there." Billy placed another log on the fire. His stomach growled. Maybe Frenchy had brought along some food. He checked the pocket and found a small leather bag tied tightly with a leather string. "What's this?"

"Gold dust. Take it," Frenchy said. "Was a small portion of my share. Was going to use it for the ranch, but I want you to have it." He looked up at Billy with sad, desperate eyes. "There's more where that came from. Last summer eight of us stopped a stage from Virginia City. Took nearly a hundred fifty thousand dollars in gold dust, bullion, diamonds. Five men were killed, including passengers and the shotgun guard."

Billy felt too stunned to say anything. He kept thinking of the bullet-riddled bodies he had seen in the stagecoach. "What . . . what happened to the other outlaws?"

"Two were captured and executed by vigilantes. Rest escaped. Some hid out west. Others went east again."

"And the loot?"

"Too heavy to carry and outrun a posse. It was split up and buried, mostly in this canyon. That's why Rock wanted to come back." Frenchy paused. He gritted his teeth. "Jim Locket—he was the brains. Said he had a map of the Ninth Gate showing where the loot was buried."

"Ninth Gate?"

"That's what we called Portneuf."

*The Ninth Gate.* Billy remembered Jackson and Rock talking about something like that the night Rock left. "So you all met up here on a certain day to dig up your share?" Billy asked.

Frenchy nodded. "Only Locket's map was wrong. Wasn't any gold."

"Why'd you attack that stagecoach?"

"Rock and the others was mad when we couldn't find the loot," Frenchy whispered. "They did it for sport. I never fired a shot."

Billy had heard Frenchy tell so many outrageous lies, he didn't know whether to believe him. "What about Jackson?"

"Helped with the holdup last summer. Guess he changed his mind about coming back to the canyon for his share. Maybe he got cold feet. Or maybe he's smarter than he looks." Frenchy paused and took a labored breath. "What happened to Owens and the others?"

Billy explained about the search for the lost horse, how he'd hurt his leg, and how the wagon train had left without him. "They're probably on their way toward the Ross Fork and the Snake River by now."

Frenchy clicked his tongue. "What a sorry outfit. Abandoning their best bullwhacker."

"You were their best bullwhacker," Billy said, "before you deserted."

"Indeed I was," Frenchy said, and smiled. He winced and his grin vanished. "You gotta make me a promise."

"What?"

"Promise you'll flag down the first wagon or stage heading

north. You pay them with that gold dust and go on to Virginia City."

Billy picked up the small leather bag and held it in his palm. The bag felt surprisingly heavy. "What about you?"

"I ain't gonna make it. In a few hours the posse will be through here. If I don't get hanged, Locket will hunt me down. He'll hunt you, too, if he thinks you might know something. You got your whole future ahead of you. You're too young for the gallows."

"I didn't do anything wrong."

"That don't make a bit of difference to an angry posse. You think they care about fair trials? Not on your life. You helped an outlaw. That's reason enough. They'll string you up soon as they get done with me. They'll be here any minute."

Billy placed the bag on the ground and stared at the fire. "I can't take your money," he said. "And I'm not going to leave you here alone."

"Don't be mulish!" Frenchy said. "Go on and get! This is your chance. You came all this way to find your father. So find him."

Frenchy's offer was tempting, Billy had to admit. He was going to have to find somebody to give him a ride the rest of the way to Virginia City. Getting a doctor to set his ankle would cost money. He'd need food, a place to sleep. How would he pay? He picked up the bag of gold dust and felt the heft of it in his hand again. The valise, the photograph—everything he owned was gone. All he had were the clothes on his back and a bum rifle. He was worse off now than when he'd left Saint Joe.

The fire crackled and popped. Billy sat upright, startled.

How much time did he have to get away? He struggled to his feet and looked down at Frenchy, who had fallen asleep. Each time he snored, his mangy white whiskers trembled. He looked as helpless as an ancient baby. *Leave now,* Billy told himself, pocketing the bag of gold dust. *Won't even have to pain yourself with good-bye.*

As Billy hobbled toward the opening, Scoundrel whined softly. Billy paused. The dog looked up at him with beseeching eyes. "Where do I think I'm going?" Billy whispered. "None of your dang business." Scoundrel cocked his head. His tail thumped.

Billy's shoulders sagged. He knew he couldn't do it. If he ran off, he'd be abandoning Frenchy. *Just like my father left me.*

"Old fool," Billy muttered to himself. "Miserable old forgivable fool."

Scoundrel's ears stood upright. He leaped to his feet and began to bark. "Roo-roo-roooo-roooo!"

Somebody was coming. From the south came the distant sound of bells.

Billy hurried outside and hobbled and hopped along the snowy road. The dog followed him to the overturned stagecoach, which was shrouded now with a layer of white. The high-pitched jangling rang louder and louder. Scoundrel's fur flared on his back. "Roo-roo-rooo-rooo!"

Billy reached into his pocket and pulled out the Colt. He pulled back the hammer and looked down the gun barrel. *Clean.* Every bullet he'd inserted was still in its chamber. Frenchy hadn't lied. The Colt had not been fired.

Billy leaned on the rifle crutch and aimed the pistol with a shaking hand in the direction of the pealing bells, which grew stronger and stronger.

*Steady. Steady.*

Two horses wearing sleigh bells burst into view pulling a sledlike contraption heaped with crates. The heavyset driver, in a dark hat and a thick black coat, pulled on the reins and brought the team to a stop. "Please throw down your gun, sir," Billy called.

"Who the hell are you?" the driver shouted in a husky voice. "Some kind of bandit? You responsible for this stagecoach accident?"

Billy gulped. "No, sir. I said throw down your gun."

The driver ignored him, knotted the reins, and leaped from the sled, which appeared to be a wagon rigged with sled runners attached to the wheels. "Looks like Locket's been here," the driver said, inspecting the stagecoach. "How many dead this time?"

"Three." Billy slowly lowered the pistol. "Plus the driver. I counted them."

"What happened to your leg?"

"Fell while I was trying to find a runaway horse. Came upon the robbery by accident," Billy said. He scanned the road in both directions for signs of approaching horsemen. He had to think quickly. "My father . . . ," he started. "My father's hurt pretty bad."

The driver sniffed. "Was wondering where that campfire smoke came from."

Billy glanced nervously toward the cave. *Never should have lit that fire.* "Please, please can you help us?"

"Why should I? I got eighty dozen eggs to carry north to Bannack. And eggs don't keep. You know what a miner will pay for a fresh egg? Small fortune."

Billy took a deep breath and pulled the gold from his pocket. "Look, sir, you can have the whole bag if you hide us in your sled. We're in an awful hurry."

The broad-faced, whiskerless driver studied Billy with piercing blue eyes. "Posse's on the way. You're too polite to be one of Locket's men. Can't tell anymore what's worse. Vigilantes or outlaws."

"Yes, sir."

"I must be crazy to do this," the driver muttered, pocketing the gold dust. "If we get stopped, I do all the talking. Understand? The dog rides in front with me. You and your father are going to have to hide under a canvas tarp in back. We need to move fast, boy. Where is he?"

Billy gulped. "Follow me."

Frenchy was lying perfectly still when they entered the cave. "Is he dead?" Billy asked, his voice quavering.

The driver took a quick look at the wound. "Humph," the driver said, and leaned over to hoist Frenchy by his armpits. "He's alive. Smother that fire best you can." Just then the driver's broad hat fell off and a long gray braid tumbled into view. "What you staring at?"

Billy felt so startled he was speechless. "Sorry, sorry . . . ma'am," he said. He averted his gaze by concentrating on kicking dirt into the last embers. "I didn't know you was a woman."

"Name's Bella. Now, grab my hat, son. Shake a leg."

Bella replaced her hat and hauled Frenchy to the sled. She

carefully shifted the crates, dumped Frenchy into a cleared spot on one side, and covered him with a canvas tarp. "Hop in," she told Billy. He did as he was told. He lay perfectly still as she threw a tarp over him, then balanced more crates atop him. "You jiggle this crate and break one egg, and your name is mud, hear me?"

"Yes, ma'am."

She whistled to Scoundrel, who leaped eagerly to the seat beside her, and they set off down the road, bells jangling. Billy's leg ached miserably. Every jounce, every jolt, seemed to rocket straight into his back, but he did not move. His greatest fear was that Frenchy would wake up, start hollering, and ruin every-thing.

Just as Bella had predicted, they weren't on the road for more than a few miles before Billy heard the sound of thunder-ing horse hooves. "Halt! Where you headed?" a familiar, chill-ing voice shouted.

*Rock!*

Billy lay perfectly still, barely able to breathe.

"Bannack," Bella said. "Carrying eggs, same as always. I'm in a hurry, so I'd appreciate it if you boys move out of my way."

Another deep voice suddenly chimed in. "Where'd you get the dog, Bella?"

"Found him a ways back, Jim. Wandering around lonesome near that stagecoach. Terrible accident. Felt sorry for him, so I took him with me. You know I'm a sucker for dogs."

"You ain't seen a fat, old, ugly man, have you?" Rock's voice demanded.

"Fat, old, ugly man? No, just this dog. Look, boys, I'd love to stay and chat, but I've got to get moving. You should do likewise. I heard there's a posse coming this way. Plummer's itching to string somebody up."

There was a sudden lurch. Billy felt the sled runners bite the snow again. Harness bells jangled. Bella whistled to the team and they set off at a faster pace. Billy's hands and feet were numb, but he felt lucky to be alive. It seemed a kind of miracle that Frenchy was still asleep.

Abruptly the sled stopped again. The bells grew silent. Horses snorted and stomped nearby. Spurs jangled. Billy held his breath. "Bella!" announced a man with an oily voice. "The prettiest egg lady this side of the Rockies."

"Where you been, Henry?" Bella scolded. "There's a stagecoach overturned near Roost Creek with three dead men shot to bits inside. What kind of lawman are you? Your posse sure took its sweet time."

"Sorry, ma'am."

"You want people in Bannack to vote for you, you better improve your record. I have half a mind to write a letter to the editor and speak my 'pinion. My customers cast ballots, you know."

"Yes, ma'am."

"Now, get out of my way. I'm in a hurry to get these eggs north. I don't have any time to waste with bumblers the likes of you."

"Yes, ma'am."

Billy squinched his eyes shut as the sled began to slide forward again. *How far?* He prayed they'd not be stopped again. Bella's performance had been remarkable. Even Scoundrel had cooperated. But could they do it again? Billy shifted the egg crate slightly, terrified he might break any of the precious cargo. Gradually, as the sled bumped along, he dozed off.

When the sled finally stopped again, Billy felt a sudden blast of light blinding him. The moldy-smelling canvas had been pulled away from his face. He blinked.

"Get out," Bella said in a low voice. "We're at Ross Creek Station. My friends will take care of you. Doc Mills usually works on horses, but he knows how to set folks' bones. You'll need to light out of here as soon as you can."

Billy had trouble sitting up. He poked Frenchy.

"Tell that remarkable woman," Frenchy said in a muffled voice from beneath the second tarp, "I need a drink."

As soon as Scoundrel heard Frenchy speak, he began leaping and barking with joy. Bella ripped the canvas from Frenchy. "Get your drink yourself."

Billy gasped. "What are you doing, ma'am? He's mortally wounded—"

"Mortally wounded, my eye!" Bella declared. "He's got a slight flesh wound. Get up, you blackguard, and help this young man. He saved your life. You should be grateful for what your son did for you."

"My son?" Frenchy said bashfully.

"That's what he told me," Bella replied. "He said he was your son."

Frenchy blinked. Then, carefully, he placed Billy's arm over his neck and helped him slide out of the wagon onto his feet. "Thank you, Billy."

Billy's face flushed bright red. "Wasn't much," he said,

thinking better of trying to explain just then what he'd done. With Frenchy's help he stumbled along toward the clearing. "Were . . . were you just pretending?"

"I meant every word," Frenchy insisted. "I am indeed grateful."

"About being hurt, I mean. How come you told me you were mortally wounded?"

"I *was* very uncomfortable. And I did lose a great deal of blood. It was a heroic gunfight. Six-shooters blazing. I deserve a medal of honor. Watch your step, Scoundrel."

Billy shook his head fondly. *Same old Frenchy.* "Sounds like you must be feeling better."

"Hurry up, now!" Bella shouted from the doorway of a low log cabin. "I've got to get back on the road."

"She's a wonder, ain't she?" Frenchy said. "Think there are many more like her in Virginia City?"

"Maybe," Billy said, filled with unexpected happiness. *The search isn't over.* No matter what happened, no matter what he discovered about his father, he suddenly understood that the journey had been worth it.

"Once we get you fixed up good and strong, you'll be able to run like the wind again," Frenchy said. "Then we'll be on our way, you bet."

Billy smiled. "You bet."

WHEN TIMES WERE HARD IN THE EAST—WHEN THERE WERE
TOO MANY CHILDREN TO SHARE THE NEW ENGLAND FARM—
WHEN YOU LEFT THE ARMY AFTER SERVING THROUGH A
WAR, AND WERE RESTLESS AND FOOTLOOSE—WHEN YOU HAD
A BROKEN HEART, OR TOO MUCH AMBITION FOR YOUR OWN
GOOD—THERE WAS ALWAYS THE WEST.

—WILLIAM HENRY JACKSON,
*TIME EXPOSURE, THE*
*AUTOBIOGRAPHY OF WILLIAM*
*HENRY JACKSON*

# Author's Note

The overland journey across the American West abounds in stories of bravery and cowardice, generosity and greed, heroism and selfishness. *Seeing the elephant* became a popular phrase beginning in the mid-1800s onward that signified going west. The elephant symbolized the Great Adventure, and all the deadly perils that confronted the untold thousands of emigrants who staked their lives and fortunes to travel to territories in what is now Colorado, Utah, Oregon, New Mexico, and California. They came in search of land, gold or silver, or a chance to start fresh in the Land of Begin Again.

Luckily, young and old alike who participated in this great western exodus from 1843 to 1870 seemed to sense the importance of their undertaking. They recorded their impressions in letters, daily diaries, newspaper and magazine accounts, and, later, reminiscences. The volume of material is astounding. Only in the recorded "folk literature" of the Civil War is there more material written by ordinary eyewitnesses.

When I began working on this historical novel, I found one brief journal entry especially intriguing. It was written May 9, 1846, by ailing twenty-three-year-old Francis Parkman. Parkman was traveling on the Oregon Trail to regain his health and record his impressions, which would later be used to create his classic, *The California and Oregon Trail*. Parkman wrote: "CW of St. Louis, who harnessed his mule into his wagons, and drove off for Santa Fe, bent on seeing. He seemed about eighteen years old, open, enterprising, and thoughtless. He will come back a full grown man."

Who was CW? Why was he leaving? And what happened to him? These were questions I found fascinating. Parkman's brief entry gave me only a tantalizing glimpse of an entire generation of young Americans who embarked on the Great Adventure to see the elephant. Some succeeded. Others did not. The journey, however, undoubtedly changed their lives forever.

In writing this novel I found especially helpful the diaries of many different travelers. One of these individuals was British scholar, adventurer, and diplomat Sir Richard F. Burton. In 1860 Burton traversed the Oregon Trail with a rifle, a brace of revolvers, a bowie knife, a top hat, a morning coat, and a silk umbrella. Other lesser-known and less flamboyantly dressed diarists included Wisconsin native Julius C. Birge, a Civil War veteran who went west with several friends in 1866. Youthful James Knox Polk Miller wrote about his experiences after he ran away from his home in Ohio in 1865 to seek his fortune in

Virginia City, Montana Territory. Another helpful diarist was twenty-six-year-old Thomas Alfred Creigh from Pennsylvania, a clerk who traveled with a disaster-prone bullwhacking team to Virginia City in 1866.

The bullwhacking experiences of twenty-three-year-old William Henry Jackson provided detailed insights into this lesser-known but critical form of western transportation. In the nineteenth century, bullwhacking teams were the modern equivalent of cross-country semitruck caravans. These operations provided young men who had little money and less experience a chance to travel across the plains as drivers or teamsters.

Jackson, who lived to be ninety-nine, kept diaries throughout his long and productive life. He recorded his impressions of his 1866 journey from New York to Salt Lake City in fascinating detail. In Denver I was fortunate to be able to examine firsthand Jackson's early, worn leather-bound pocket-size diaries crammed with notes and pencil sketches. These have been preserved by the State Historical Society of Colorado.

Jackson, who became a premier Western landscape photographer, sketched some of his earliest impressions of the West in these notebooks. Much later, when he was in his eighties, he returned to these notebooks to create sketches for mural-size paintings of the American westward movement. He was hired by the National Park Service to paint these images, which were displayed in Washington, D.C.

Like Jackson's paintings, the folklore of the West continues to be an inspiring but often confounding source of information. In researching my historical novel I discovered many conflicting facts about the 1865 Portneuf Canyon stagecoach robbery in Bannock County, Idaho. What happened to the loot remains a mystery. The gold, which may have been split up among the band of robbers, is believed to have been hidden but never recovered. Somewhere in the canyon, folklore says, a sizable fortune remains buried.

# About the Author

LAURIE LAWLOR has published more than thirty books for children and young adults, including *Dead Reckoning: A Pirate's Voyage with Captain Drake. Magnificent Voyage: An American Adventurer on Captain James Cook's Final Expedition* was on *VOYA's* Nonfiction Honor List and was called "fascinating" by the *New York Times. Helen Keller: Rebellious Spirit* was named an American Library Association Notable Book and a Best Book for Young Adults. *Shadow Catcher: The Life and Work of Edward S. Curtis* won a Golden Kite Honor Award and the Carl Sandburg Award. Ms. Lawlor lives in Evanston, Illinois.